"So we're ba...

"Can't seem to get away from it, can we?" Sam's eyes darkened with a need that matched the ache inside her. "We definitely have a problem and we're going to have to deal with it sooner or later."

"Oh?" His fingers on her cheek made it difficult to speak. "How so?"

He inched closer. "We both have this need to find out whether we're as good together as we used to be."

That could be dangerous, she wanted to say, but could only nod.

"Just one kiss, and then we can put this misplaced attraction behind us."

Maybe he had a point. It would be nice to move past the unwanted desire that kept her awake at night and on edge by day. "All right. But just one kiss."

Standing on her toes, she rose to meet him. His eyelids drifted shut and, released from the spell of his gaze, she panicked. *This is a terrible mistake!*

Then his lips touched hers, and she was lost.

Dear Reader,

When I was six my mother signed me up for ballet lessons because I was clumsy. Being a warm and nurturing woman, she never told me this. She simply enrolled me, then brought home pink slippers, white tights and a black leotard. One look at those slippers and I was sold. I loved everything surrounding dance: the music, the scuffed hardwood floor, the other kids and watching the teacher demonstrate various leg and arm positions. But a dancer I'm not. I failed miserably at it and, alas, quit after a few months. Luckily, as I matured, I grew out of the clumsy stage. (Though from time to time I still trip over things, usually when I'm preoccupied with a story I'm working on.)

Despite my failure as a dancer, I have always loved the ballet, both professional and amateur. So naturally, the heroine of this story, Amy Parker, is a former ballerina. She and Sam Cutter, an entrepreneur, married quite young. Theirs was a passionate union filled with misunderstandings and arguments. Unfortunately the marriage lasted less than a year, leaving them both bitter and hurt. This story opens twelve years later. Amy teaches ballet to children. Sam's niece is enrolled in her school. *The Last Time We Kissed* is the heartwarming story of Sam and Amy's reconciliation.

This is my first Harlequin American Romance novel, and I'm excited to share it with you. I hope you enjoy reading it as much as I enjoyed writing it.

Sincerely,

Ann Roth

THE LAST TIME WE KISSED

Ann Roth

TORONTO • NEW YORK • LONDON
AMSTERDAM • PARIS • SYDNEY • HAMBURG
STOCKHOLM • ATHENS • TOKYO • MILAN • MADRID
PRAGUE • WARSAW • BUDAPEST • AUCKLAND

To my agent, Pam Hopkins.
Thanks for your continued encouragement and support.

Special thanks to Lynn Beasley for her help about running
a ballet school for children, and for patiently answering
my questions. Any mistakes or misinformation are mine.

ISBN 0-373-75035-8

THE LAST TIME WE KISSED

Copyright © 2004 by Ann Roth.

www.eHarlequin.com

Printed in U.S.A.

ABOUT THE AUTHOR

Ann Roth has always been a voracious reader, reading everything from classics to mysteries to romance. Of all the books she's read, love stories affected her the most, and stayed with her the longest. A firm believer in the power of love, Ann enjoys creating emotional stories that illustrate how love can triumph over seemingly insurmountable odds.

Ann lives in the greater Seattle area with her husband and a really irritating cat who expects her breakfast no later than 6:00 a.m., seven days a week.

She would love to hear from readers. You can write her c/o P.O. Box 25003, Seattle, WA 98165-1903 or e-mail her at ATROTH@comcast.net.

Chapter One

AMY PARKER strode to the middle of the stage and clapped her hands. "Attention, Pearls!"

A dozen six-, seven- and eight-year-old children clustered on the benches along the wall swiveled from the room-length mirror toward her, while Kari Jeffries, the mother whose turn it was to help out and provide the snack, held a warning finger to her lips.

"Rehearsal starts in ten minutes," Amy said. "Please get ready." She glanced at her assistant of the day. "Mrs. Jeffries, will you help?"

Kari nodded, her chin-length hair swinging forward. Excited chatter erupted and filled the air as some children exchanged their street shoes for ballet slippers, while others warmed up at the barre adjacent to the benches. Amy inserted a well-used CD into the player and then set the remote on top of the notebook containing her choreography notes. As founder of the Amy Parker School of Dance, the brand-new Forest Hills, Washington, ballet school for grade- and middle-school children, she looked forward to the first annual end-of-the-year performance. With only five weeks to go, the Pearls, Emeralds and Rubies were rehearsing daily, though in separate groups. The next hour belonged to the Pearls.

They were all here except for Mariah Carlson. Amy wasn't worried. The eight-year-old was one of her most enthusiastic pupils. She wouldn't miss—

Suddenly the door at the dimly lit back of the room opened. A slice of afternoon sunlight briefly illuminated the diminutive Mariah, who hurried inside, followed by a male too tall and muscular to be her father. He moved with a fluid grace at odds with his size, his step as familiar to Amy as her favorite leotard.

For a moment, the room and everyone in it seemed to fade as recognition jolted through her. *No, it can't be.* But even as her mind denied the truth, her heart knew.

Sam Cutter had just entered her dance studio.

Amy tried to swallow but her throat had gone dry. She shouldn't have been surprised. For weeks, she'd known that he would be looking after Mariah while the girl's parents enjoyed a three-week cruise. She'd psyched herself up for this meeting, had assured herself she could handle it. But she hadn't expected to see Sam quite so soon.

Mariah waved. Amy's hands and legs began to

shake, and only her years of rigorous training kept her from collapsing in a helpless wreck. Somehow, she managed a return wave and a smile.

Sam seemed equally unsettled as he hovered a few yards shy of the door, his body tense and his jaw taut. The small girl beside him pulled his hand. "Come on, Uncle Sam, I want you to meet Miss Parker."

Of course, Mariah wouldn't know they'd already met, ages before her birth. There was no reason to tell her without a round of endless questions that would only stir up a past better left buried.

Gripping the girl's small gym bag, Sam moved slowly into the windowless studio, his stride as hesitant as Amy's stuttering heart. At a loss for what to do, she snatched up her choreography notebook, opened it and pretended to scan the pages, while studying Sam from beneath lowered lashes.

He still favored T-shirts and snug, faded jeans. He'd filled out some since she'd last seen him twelve years ago, his chest broader, his arms stronger, and his body somehow bigger. *Power and steel.* The words popped into her mind, and they described him well. His hair, jet-black and as long as ever, was neatly pulled back in a ponytail. The diamond stud in his ear, which he'd worn since his senior year of high school, winked in the dim light.

He didn't appear to have changed much. A bitter smile twisted Amy's lips. No surprise there. Sam would never change, and all the love and tears in the world couldn't alter that. She gave up the pretense of scanning the notes, instead hugging the binder to her chest.

The children had stopped tugging off their sneakers to whisper among themselves and scrutinize this stranger with open interest. Kari smoothed her hair and sucked in her stomach, the way women did around a man like Sam. Sporting an oblivious smile, Mariah continued to lead her grim-faced uncle forward. A small slip of a girl eagerly dragging a great big man. It was almost laughable, or would have been under different circumstances.

At the foot of the stage, Sam balked, refusing to go any farther. His legs splayed in a stubborn stance Amy well remembered, while his jaw clamped shut and his expression darkened.

The undaunted Mariah adjusted by releasing his hand, taking her bag from him and beaming. "This is my Uncle," she proudly stated. "He's taking care of me for three whole weeks."

Somehow, Amy's ability to speak had vanished and she stood mute. Her ice-cold hands tightened on the notebook so that the cardboard cut into her palms, but she barely noticed. Sam stood not five feet in front of her. Not just a fantasy or a late-night dream, but the man himself.

Mentally she'd rehearsed this moment at least a hundred times, yet now her mind was oddly blank.

Her body, however, was in total chaos: heart pounding, nerves stretched tight, breathing shallow. With amazing speed, the familiar warmth she'd thought she'd forgotten uncurled in her stomach.

After all this time, he still had the power do that to her. Wonder, then distress shook her. Unnerved and totally confused, she lifted the thick braid that hung down her back and brought it forward while she prayed that the floor would open up beneath her feet and pull her underground and out of sight. Since that wasn't happening, she forced herself to stand tall and face him. "Hello, Sam."

He shifted uncomfortably before his robin's egg-blue eyes settled on her. He'd gotten those from his mother, a Swede, while his tawny skin and black hair came from his Native American father.

"Hello, Amy." His throat worked thickly. "It's been a long time."

Once that low, sexy voice had sent thrills shivering through her. Unfortunately, it still did. Resisting the urge to sigh, Amy schooled her expression to disinterest. "Yes, it has."

Then, silence. What was there to say? It had all been said with heated accusations and hateful words twelve years ago.

A worried frown darkened Mariah's face as she glanced from Sam to Amy. "What's the matter?"

"Nothing," Amy replied, feigning nonchalance with an airy wave. She meant that, too. There was nothing between her and Sam, had been nothing for a long time. This strong visceral reaction to him, well, it was simply because he was a powerfully built, good-looking man.

She tore her gaze from Sam's to glance at Mariah. The girl's shoulder-length brown hair hung loose around her face. "We're about to start rehearsal, so change your shoes, then hurry and fix your hair. Mrs. Jeffries will help you put it into a bun."

The little girl nodded, then scampered off, her small gym bag bumping her leg.

Sam shoved his hands into his pockets and remained planted in front of Amy, his expression indifferent except for the glint of interest in his eyes. Her stomach knotted with tension. She wanted only to get rid of him and then lose herself in her work. She made a show of glancing at the slim gold watch on her wrist. "We'll be finished by six. You can pick up Mariah then."

"Okay." He searched her face as if memorizing her features. "It's good to see you," he said, then looked surprised at his own words.

"And you," she replied before she could stop herself. *I've been back in town for a year now. Why haven't you looked me up?*

Not that she'd wanted him to. If not for Mariah, they could have coexisted in Forest Hills without ever running into each other. They didn't share the same friends or the same interests, and never had.

"I'm ready, Miss Parker," Mariah called from the bench. "See you later, Uncle Sam."

He waved goodbye, then turned around and strode to the exit as if he couldn't wait to leave.

When the door shut behind him, a wide-eyed Kari joined Amy on stage. "That was Sam Cutter, the owner of the Cutter's Fabulous Burgers chain," she said with blatant admiration. "I've seen his picture in the papers. He's even better-looking in person. How do you know him?"

"How do I know Sam?" Amy repeated, stalling for time while she corralled the whirl of emotions tumbling inside her. Kari was a world-class gossip, and Amy did not relish being the subject of her latest juicy story. She picked up the remote and pushed the play button. Strains from a lighthearted Mozart piece filled the room. She hit Pause, then offered Kari what she hoped was a dismissive smile. "I used to be married to him."

THE MOMENT SAM EASED his black Porsche from the parking lot after dance class an hour and a half later, Mariah turned to him with a scolding frown. "You didn't come in and get me."

"I waited outside, just like I said I would." The furrow between his niece's brows deepened, so he shot her a puzzled look. "You do remember our conversation?"

"Yes, but Mom always comes inside." She stuck

her hands out the open sunroof, waving her fingers through the late afternoon spring air. "I wanted you to do that, too."

"And I was supposed to know that by reading your mind?"

"No, Uncle Sam." Her freckled nose wrinkled, and she jerked her hands down to her lap. "You were supposed to open the door, walk in and get me."

Brother. "I see."

He'd thought taking care of his sister Jeannie's daughter would be a piece of cake. Boy, was he wrong. Mariah was stubborn and opinionated, a scheming female in the making, and he was beginning to realize just how hard Jeannie and Mike had it.

Sam felt like an amateur walking a tightrope, unsure how to handle his niece. He figured he'd appeal to the kid's ego. "I thought, hey, you're a mature, eight-year-old girl, and that makes you perfectly able to walk out the door and find me."

Mariah sniffed, refusing to be mollified by the flattery. "I know why you didn't come in. You don't like Miss Parker."

"Where'd you get that idea?" Sam asked, though he thought he knew the answer. His niece must have picked up on the tension between him and Amy, which had vibrated between them like an overwound spring ready to snap.

After all the time that had passed, he hadn't expected that. He shook his head. But then, he hadn't anticipated what seeing her would do to him. The woman who had once been his wife was no longer the skinny teenage girl he'd married. Sure, she still had a dancer's fit and slender body, but she was softer and fuller now. All woman, and as attractive as hell. Interest piqued him as it hadn't for a long while, and he wondered if she tasted as sweet as he remembered. He quickly dismissed the thought, setting his jaw.

Mariah had said he didn't like her teacher, but *like* was the wrong word for the strong emotions churning in his gut. His tangled feelings were impossible to capture in words. There was too much fire and pain between him and Amy. "She's okay," he said, keeping his tone neutral.

"Then why were you such a grouch around her?"

"Me, a grouch?" Sam snorted and braked for a red light. In the growing dusk, fragrant lilacs ringed with colorful tulips were still visible in the median dividing the street, but he barely noticed. "So I didn't smile or make small talk." He remembered Amy's cool expression and added, "Your teacher wasn't exactly thrilled to see me, either." Three blocks down, a brightly lit, blue-and-gold Cutter's Fabulous Burger sign rotated slowly, beckoning hungry drivers. "I'll bet you're starved. Want to grab a burger before heading home?"

"Okay. Why wasn't Miss Parker thrilled?"

Sam stifled a colorful expletive. Typical one-track mind. The kid wouldn't be satisfied until he'd answered her questions. The light turned green, and he accelerated. "That's a complicated question. Let's just say we've known each other for a while, since long before you were born."

"I didn't know that. Did you like each other then?"

He shot a glance at his niece. The interested expression on her face meant who knew how many more prying questions. Unless he satisfied her curiosity. How to explain? He considered making up a story, but that wasn't his style. The only safe route was the honest one. He'd tell her and end the matter. He shrugged. "We got married, so I guess we liked each other well enough," he said carefully, knowing Mariah could repeat this conversation to her friends and maybe to Amy.

Her eyes widened. "You and Miss Parker used to be married?" She huffed, a tiny breath fraught with scorn. "In case you didn't know, April Fool's Day was last month. It's May now."

"I'm not fooling," he replied soberly.

"You're not?" His niece gaped at him. She shrieked, then covered her mouth with her hand. "That's ultracool! You guys must have *loved* each other."

"We thought so at the time." Instead they'd confused lust for love. The lust had never faded, growing stronger each time they made love, which they'd done as often as possible. Unfortunately, sexual chemistry had been the only positive thing going for them. When they weren't tearing off each other's clothes, they fought like wildcats.

Mariah giggled. "Sam and Amy, sittin' in a tree, k-i-s-s-i-n-g..."

Sam rolled his eyes, though the silly poem brought to mind the time he and Amy *had* made love in a tree. They'd been walking through a deserted park at dusk. As often happened back then, they were so hot for each other they couldn't wait until they got home. So they'd climbed up an old, leafy maple, found the sturdiest branch, and let their passions explode. Tricky, but exciting. He'd never had sex like that again, and probably never would. The mere thought was arousing. His groin stirred. Frowning, he shifted in his seat. "Amy was barely eighteen and I was twenty, and we were too young for the responsibility. Getting married was a mistake. We divorced less than a year later."

"That's so sad," Mariah sighed in her best dramatic voice.

And so damn painful, he'd never again go the marriage route. He shrugged. "We got over it."

His niece's small arms crossed her chest indignantly, while her chin thrust up. "How come you never told *me* about this?"

"It was old news. Besides it's not important anymore. After the divorce Amy, uh, Miss Parker, moved to San Francisco and joined a ballet company. I didn't figure I'd run into her again, not even when she moved back to Forest Hills and you started dance lessons. But then your mom and dad decided to take that cruise, and I offered to take care of you, and here we are."

"Oh." Mariah chewed the pad of her thumb and fell silent, satisfied at last.

Sam heaved a sigh of relief. Thank God.

In the quiet, his thoughts turned to Amy. She'd been immersed in the rehearsal this afternoon, all serious business and no fun. Just as she'd always been.

So what if she looked better than ever? She was still the same career-oriented woman, only instead of focusing on her own dancing, she now focused completely on her students. How did he know this? For one thing, she wasn't married. He'd checked around and learned that she wasn't dating anyone, either, and hadn't since moving back to town a year ago. She spent most of her time in her studio. Dance had always been her life, more important to her than anything else. It looked as if it still was. Sam didn't fault her for having a career, but her priorities were skewed. For that reason, she didn't interest him.

"I have rehearsal every day and you have to walk me in, so you'd better be nice to her," Mariah cautioned.

Here we go again. Curbing his impatience, Sam managed to keep his tone even. "Why can't I just drop you at the door?"

"Because," she said as if he were the child and she the adult, "I'm a Pearl. You don't go in by yourself until you're an Emerald or a Ruby. I won't be an Emerald until next year when I'm nine, and I won't be a Ruby until I'm eleven."

"What about on Tuesday and Thursday, when you carpool? Don't you and your friends walk in by yourselves?"

"Not until we're Emeralds."

"I see," Sam said, though he didn't. He found Mariah's female sense of logic baffling, but not surprising. Were girls born that way? "You're lucky I run my own business. What would you do if I couldn't pick you up from school and walk you inside?"

"But you can." Her lips compressed, reminding him of her mother—his sister—and the subject was closed.

Someday his cute, little freckle-nosed niece was going to make some poor guy miserable. Sam stifled a grin.

The Cutter's Fabulous Burger sign was just ahead. He signaled and pulled into the paved lot. The place was hopping, he noted with pride. He now owned five of the fast-food restaurants—two in Forest Hills and three in the surrounding area. Unlike his failed marriage, his business just kept getting better.

Sam scowled. He didn't like to compare his marriage to his business. He didn't like to think about his marriage, period.

Yet today he'd thought about the past a lot. He'd known Amy had moved back into town. How could he not? Even if his sister hadn't told him, some radar-like system in his gut knew. Amy's effect on him was that strong, and after spending a few miserable weeks wondering whether they'd run into each other, he'd managed to squelch his tension—if he saw her, he saw her—and lock the painful memories in a dark place deep inside of him. But coming face-to-face with her had jarred him and shaken some of those memories loose.

It was the shock of seeing her for the first time since the divorce, he reasoned. He was over that now. Tomorrow was Thursday, carpool day, so he wouldn't be driving. But on Friday, he'd walk Mariah inside and he'd do it without hesitation. Seeing Amy again would have no effect on him at all.

In fact, he looked forward to facing her, just to prove that to himself.

DESPITE THE HECTIC rehearsal schedule, on Thursdays Amy closed the studio at six. Thank goodness, for today had been a Thursday from hell. At the moment, it was just after six but it felt like midnight.

As she dust-mopped the stage in preparation for tomorrow, the day's chaotic events played through her mind.

The morning had gone smoothly enough, just the usual paperwork and finishing the sketches for the recital's four simple but work-intensive sets. The problems had started this afternoon. Bobby Jarrett, one of the six boys in the Emerald group, had arrived early, in the middle of the Rubies rehearsal. Bored with waiting for his group's turn on stage, he'd clowned around and jammed his big toe. That required a call to his mother, who had whisked her white-faced ten-year-old off to the doctor. Then the Tchaikovsky CD the Ruby group practiced to had begun to skip, apparently worn out from overuse. They'd had to rehearse without music. That had thrown many of them into confusion, which meant they didn't know their parts as well as Amy had thought. So they'd run through the routine until the dancers seemed more sure of themselves, which had thrown off the schedule for the rest of the afternoon.

As if that weren't enough, Molly Andrews and Sabrina Rollins, both Emeralds and among the group's most promising ballerinas, had gotten into a big fight over who was the better dancer. Amy had taken more time away from rehearsal to play referee, soothing both ruffled egos by pointing out that they were equally good.

She stopped mopping to pick up a Band-Aid wrapper, from when Tammy Martin, an Emerald, discovered a blister on her pinkie toe. Not from her dancing slippers, but from the too-tight but fashionable shoes she'd worn all day in school. Amy needed to replenish the Band-Aid supply and buy a replacement CD on her way home tonight. "Band-Aids and CD," she proclaimed aloud, to help her remember.

On top of all that, she'd started the day exhausted. She yawned, and her tired eyes watered. She hadn't slept well last night, partly due to the stress of this whole end-of-year dance production. Yes, they were children, and no one expected perfection. Yet because her school was not quite a year old and this was the first recital, she wanted it to be good. But the reason she'd tossed and turned had less to do with her school and more to do with Sam Cutter. Seeing him yesterday had totally unnerved her.

Which was thoroughly aggravating, as well as confusing. Mop in hand, Amy descended the three steps leading to the stage. She shook the mop head over the trash receptacle, absently watching the debris float silently into the can. She was over the man, yet one brief meeting had stirred up a tumultuous mix of desire, bitterness and heartache, along with a pang of longing. Emotions she'd dealt with and dismissed years ago, or thought she had. Apparently not.

She slid the mop over the polished wood floor

surrounding the barre and bench areas. All day, she'd wondered what she would have done if he'd walked through the door again this afternoon. Thankfully, Mariah had come in with Jessica Stevens, Meggie Markus and Jessica's mother. The girl hadn't even mentioned Sam. Which was a relief, Amy told herself, even if she had anticipated seeing him. The thought brought a frown to her face. Only to show him how little he affected her, she assured herself as she returned the mop to the closet.

She rubbed her hip, which ached, the result of an injury that had cut short her career as a dancer. Her empty stomach growled loudly. With all the commotion today, she'd been too busy to eat lunch. Ravenous, she slipped into her ballet-pink cardigan. She grabbed her purse and the canvas bag she used to transport her choreography notebook and other items she needed at home. After one last glance around the studio, she flipped off the lights and slipped through the door. The dead bolt clicked behind her.

The parking lot abutting the building was empty except for her Volkswagen Beetle, its banana-yellow color adding a bright note to the drab asphalt. Amy headed toward the car, pulling in a breath of flower-scented air as she walked. Instantly she felt better. She hadn't had much chance to enjoy the unusually pleasant weather, and just being outside refreshed her. She stowed her bag in the trunk. The sun was about to set, and through a gap between two twelve-story buildings across the street she noted the streaks of crimson that colored the darkening sky. It was a beautiful, clear spring evening, though on the cool side. She hugged her cardigan close and decided to walk the six blocks to Betty Jean's Coffee Hut, which served excellent food and was one of her favorite places. After the meal she'd walk back and pick up her car. She needed the fresh air and besides, walking was good for her hip.

Amy set off. There were lots of people out and about, and she nodded and smiled at familiar faces and strangers alike. Forest Hills had always been a friendly town. She'd missed the close-knit community and was glad to be back. The only bad part about it was that Sam lived here, too.

She frowned. She'd managed to avoid the man for nearly a year. Once Mariah's parents returned from vacation, she'd be able to avoid him again.

With firm determination she drove the man from her thoughts and focused on her surroundings. She was less than a block from the gray cinder block Forest Hills Library and just two blocks from Betty Jean's. Several of her students were in the library tonight, she knew, working on school projects just as she had throughout grade and high school. In fact, she'd first met Sam at that library. She frowned again. Why did she keep thinking about him?

Suddenly, as if her question had tempted the fates,

there he was, heading straight toward her. Her heart gave a funny kick, and without realizing it she stopped right in the middle of the sidewalk. She knew exactly when he spotted her. His brow lifted, registering surprise, and his step faltered. It wasn't yet dark, and even from twenty feet away she could make out the pale blue of his eyes. As he continued toward her, those eyes lit and hooked her. She couldn't look away.

Awareness jolted through her, followed swiftly by self-disgust. She jerked her attention to the stubborn jut of his chin. Unless she was a total fool, she had no business being attracted to Sam Cutter.

As he drew closer she couldn't resist another glance at him. A furrow of displeasure marred his smooth forehead. Then vanished as his gaze roved boldly over her with a singular, intimate heat that drove every negative thought from her mind. She drew in a shaky, shallow breath. A fine tension hummed through her body, and suddenly she felt like the awestruck sixteen-year-old girl she'd been when they'd first met.

With stark honesty, she admitted the truth: she'd thought yesterday's strong physical reaction to Sam was a onetime thing, that she was now immune to him. Well, she'd thought wrong. After all these years, he had only to look at her and her insides turned to putty.

She didn't have to like it, but there it was. Amy

stiffened her spine. Sam Cutter was the last person
she needed in her life. She would fight her attraction with all her strength—no matter what her thud-
ding heart wanted.

Chapter Two

SAM COULD HARDLY believe his eyes. Amy stood less than twenty feet away, her expression shadowed in the gathering dusk. He swore silently. She was the last person he wanted to see, and he considered offering a terse nod and ducking into the library, where Mariah awaited him. Unfortunately, his legs disagreed and strode straight toward Amy. All right, he'd say hello and then leave.

Her arms hugged her waist as if she were cold. She wore clogs, loose turquoise overalls, a white T-shirt, and a sweater the same pale pink as ballet slippers. He couldn't even see her shape in those clothes. So why did his blood stir as if she were wearing some tight, slinky dress?

Irritated at his reaction, which was unwelcome, unwanted and unsettling, he scowled as he stopped half a foot in front of her. "Shouldn't you be at your studio, working?"

"Hello to you, too." She clutched her extra-large

shoulder bag close, hugging it, and matched his unhappy expression with one of her own. "Didn't Mariah tell you? On Thursdays, the studio closes at six."

"She told me, but I didn't believe it." His arms crossed over his chest. "It's not like you to take time off." His mouth curled in a humorless smile. "Ever."

He knew by the shock on her face that she remembered their arguments over that very point and that she didn't appreciate his comment.

Bristling, she lifted her head high. "For your information, I do have a life outside the studio. At the moment I happen to be on my way to Betty Jean's," she replied stiffly, as if that proved her statement.

Sam wondered if she were meeting some guy there. His gut tensed at the thought, and a cold, empty feeling filled his chest. Shoving his hands in the rear pockets of his jeans, he rocked back on his heels. Her love life was none of his concern. "The food at Cutter's is better," he said with pride.

"Cutter's is great, but I wanted a place within walking distance of the studio. You've done well with your business, Sam."

High praise coming from Amy. He dipped his head in acknowledgment of the compliment. He wanted her to approve of what he'd accomplished, and her remark pleased him. "Thanks."

"You're welcome." Her expression softened as she met his eye.

"Are you meeting someone at Betty Jean's?" he blurted out. He bit back a silent oath. *Real smooth, Cutter.* Yet he couldn't help following up with another question. "A date, maybe?"

Her eyes widened as if the question caught her by surprise. "Not that it's any of your business, but no. With the upcoming recital, I'm too busy to date."

He nodded, disliking the relief that sluiced through him. Two preteen girls stopped midway up the library steps, clutching notebooks and chattering excitedly. "Hi, Miss Parker!" they called in unison.

"Hello, girls."

The streetlights blinked on, illuminating Amy's face. Her eyes seemed to sparkle as she waved at the girls, who stared openly at Sam.

"Hi, Mr. Cutter," they shouted, and he realized they were students he'd met at Amy's dance school.

"Hey there." He winked, and they giggled with pleasure. They dashed up the remaining steps and disappeared inside.

Amy turned back to him with a questioning frown. "Where's Mariah tonight?"

He gestured at the library. "I'm on my way to pick her up."

That earned him a sharp look. "You let her go by herself? She's only eight years old," she accused in an outraged tone that grated on his nerves.

"Eight going on thirty," Sam quipped, but she

didn't smile. He stiffened. "You make me sound like a criminal."

She tilted her chin, so that the streetlight cast her eyes in shadow. "Well, you ought to know better."

"I'm not stupid, Amy. Mariah went to the library with a couple of friends."

"Oh. Why didn't you say that in the first place?" Tiny vertical lines appeared between her eyebrows. "Your communication skills sure haven't improved any."

Her expression of superiority really bugged him. "You and I used to communicate pretty damn well," he drawled, just to shake the attitude out of her. "Especially in bed."

Though dusk was fast turning to night, he noted the red flush sweeping her face. The smug tilt of her mouth straightened. Sam experienced his own smug feeling. *Score one for me.*

He was right, too. They'd understood each other's bodies and physical needs as well as their own. Though a sweater and overalls concealed Amy's shape, he let his gaze drift familiarly over her. To the sweet curve where her neck joined her shoulder, then lower, to her small, proud breasts with the dusky rose nipples, so sensitive that they hardened and stood at attention at the lightest touch...

He cleared his throat and yanked his gaze to her face. Her eyes were soft and her breathing shallow as if she, too, remembered how it had been between them. Heat flared in Sam's belly and groin. He swallowed back a groan.

"Only in bed," Amy retorted, hugging her purse to her chest like a protective shield.

He snickered. "As I remember it, we 'communicated' in plenty of places besides bed. On the kitchen table, in the shower, leaning against the door, for starters." Her face was crimson now. He snapped his mouth shut. What had gotten into him?

"Sa-a-am," she wailed with exasperation. "Can't you ever be serious?"

The angry glint in her eyes and tight press of her lips warned that he was pushing her to the limits of her composure. But he couldn't seem to stop. "As I remember it, your idea of 'serious' is an argument." A sound of protest issued from her throat. She opened her mouth to speak, but he pushed on. "Do you still do that? Drive a guy insane with your do-it-my-way-or-else agenda?"

Up came her chin, and her fist balled tightly on her hip. "Talk about skewing the picture. You were the controlling one, and you know it." She tossed her head, making her thick braid swish and swing, and Sam knew her next words would pack a sting. "No wonder you're still single."

He'd been right. *Direct hit from Amy.* "I'm single because I choose to be," he said. Which was the so-help-me-God truth. It was her sarcastic, yet pitying, tone that smarted. "You're not married, either," he pointed out.

"True." Regret flickered in her eyes. "But hopefully that's going to change."

Had he heard wrong, then? Was she serious with someone? For some reason the thought soured his mood further. He couldn't stop his scowl. "Who's the lucky guy?"

"We haven't met yet. I'm just saying, I'm ready to settle down and start a family."

Sam didn't like the relief her statement caused. "With your workaholic habits?" He studied her in disbelief. "I don't see it happening."

She shot him an exasperated look. "This is the twenty-first century, Sam. Women can have families *and* careers, and do both successfully." She shot him a sad look. "You never did understand that."

"Neither did you," he said. Her jaw dropped, and he knew he was treading dangerous waters.

"Hey, Mr. Cutter," a young girl called from the top step of the library. "Mariah's waiting for you at the checkout desk," she said, staring at him and Amy with open curiosity.

"Thanks," he said, then returned his attention to Amy. "Look, I don't want to fight with you. We did enough of that while we were married. For Mariah's sake, we ought to try to get along. It's only for three weeks, until her parents come home."

Amy pulled in a breath and blew it out, as if

working to calm herself. Her shoulders lost some of their defensive rigidity. "You're right," she agreed, sounding rational now. "The past is past, and we should keep it that way."

"So we have a truce?"

"It won't be easy, but I'll do my best. Truce."

She'd agreed with him. That was a first. Sam tried not to let it go to his head, and only with force did he bite back a gloating retort. "Great," he said instead. He extended his hand to shake on it.

She stared at his outstretched arm for a few uncomfortable moments. Just when he was about to give up and drop his hand, she extended her own. Though her hand was small and fine-boned, her grip was firm, a business person's shake. Yet fresh heat climbed up his arm and spread to his groin. After all these years, her skin was still smooth and soft. He couldn't stifle the need to caress the delicate underside of her wrist with his thumb.

Amy's pulse jumped under his touch. Awareness darkened her caramel-colored eyes. Suddenly she gasped, as if she'd just realized the electricity flowing between them and didn't like it.

Neither did Sam. They broke contact at the same time, quickly backing away from each other. Amy averted her gaze, staring into the distance.

"You have a good evening," she said, already on her way.

Sam gave a terse nod. "Back at ya."

Keen to get inside and forget about her, he strode purposefully up the library steps. *Running away like a coward,* a voice in his head jeered. Sam's jaw tightened. He was no coward, and this wasn't running away.

Maybe he wanted another look at the woman who had once been his wife. Or maybe he needed to prove to himself that he wasn't running. Whatever the reason he stopped short of the door and pivoted around. It was nearly dark now, but the streetlights allowed him to watch Amy. She moved quickly, agile as a cat from years of dance training. Sam thought about her feet with the high arches and taped toes, blistered and sore from hours of dancing in uncomfortable toe shoes. Yet so beautiful, like works of art. And her legs, smooth and shapely as only a dancer's are. She was only five feet four inches to his six-two, but when her thighs gripped his hips, those legs seemed impossibly long…

A low moan tore from his throat, and he was grateful no one was around to hear. Dammit, he would *not* think of her as anything more than Mariah's teacher. He jerked open the door and strode inside.

Yet even as he girded his will and set his mind to obey, he knew that it was going to be a long three weeks.

WHILE THE CLAWFOOT TUB filled later that Thursday evening, Amy hung a clean nightgown and terry-cloth robe on the brass hook she'd screwed into the door of her sixty-year-old bathroom. Then she struck a match and lit the wicks of the six fat vanilla-scented candles that lined the windowsill, each in its own wrought-iron saucer. A fusion jazz CD played softly on the portable disk player. She stepped out of her clothes, tucking them into the wicker hamper, and then turned off the mock Tiffany light overhead.

The steaming tub was full now, and her bath preparations complete. Just as she turned off the water, the phone, which she'd placed on an old green, yellow and red footstool she'd hand-stenciled, rang. She knew who that was—her two oldest and closest friends, Nina and Dani. Nina had three-way calling on her phone, and while Amy had lived and danced in San Francisco, the three had connected via phone several times a week. Now that she'd moved back, they still did. She answered on the third ring, setting the system to speaker phone.

"Hello, you two." She stepped into a mound of bubbles, also vanilla-scented, then sank into the hot water with a contented sigh. "Hope you don't mind if I'm on the speaker phone tonight. What's up with the wedding plans?"

"In a minute," replied Nina, the statuesque five-foot-eleven bride-to-be. "Do I hear the splash of water? I'll bet you're in the tub."

"Is it Thursday night?" Dani quipped, and Amy pictured the wry glint in her eyes.

Amy's friends knew her rituals as well as she did, and though they couldn't see her, she smiled as she settled her head against her comfy pink tub pillow. Their obvious interest and concern were as comforting as the scented bath—totally unlike her relationship with Sam. The thought destroyed her smile.

"Yes to both questions." Her hip appreciated hot soaks in the tub, and she indulged herself whenever time permitted, which usually meant Thursday nights and Sundays. "So, Nina, did you and Ben pick out the invitations?"

"Finally," said Nina, who tended to procrastinate. "With only nine weeks before the wedding, getting the order back from the printer and mailed in time will be a real challenge. I'm going to need your help—"

"Which you'll have," Dani broke in, and Amy knew that her lips were pursed in impatience. "I'm bursting to tell you my news. You'll never guess," she said, then rushed on before they could. "We're not having one baby, we're having two. Twins!"

"Two little Libras instead of one." Nina's voice was laced with excitement, and Amy knew she was already plotting out their astrological charts. A talented owner of a dress design and alterations business, Nina had studied astrology on the side and considered herself a near expert. "Oh, how wonderful."

"Ditto," Amy said, though with less enthusiasm. She was happy for her friend, truly. Yet she couldn't stem a pang of envy. With Dani happily married and pregnant, and Nina soon to be a bride, Amy was the odd woman out. She felt it, too. Her friends had included her in every step of their personal milestones, but the truth was, she was on the outside looking in. She wanted what they had.

"Russ is nearly through the roof with excitement," Dani continued. The faint click-clack of knitting needles sounded through the speaker, and Amy knew the knitting-store owner and mother-to-be was hard at work, probably making a blanket for the second baby. "I'll be huge at your wedding, Nina."

And I'll be trim, slim and alone. Amy stifled a sigh.

"With Venus direct on that day, and my two oldest and dearest friends as bridesmaids, one of them pregnant, can things get any better?" Amy heard pages rustling, indicating that Nina was thumbing through one of her many astrology books. "According to Ben's and my charts, all the signs are right for a long, happy union." Without missing a beat, she changed the subject. "Hey, Amy, did Sam show up at your dance class today?"

Amy had told her friends about their first meeting. She almost wished she hadn't, for the very mention of his name caused her muscles to tense. But only for a moment. The steaming water quickly

eased the tightness. She frowned as she lifted her
foot from the suds and examined the callus on her
big toe. Though she no longer danced except to
demonstrate steps to her students she still had
dancer's feet, with all the lumps and bumps. Ugly.
Wrinkling her nose, she plunged her foot back under
the suds. "No, but I ran into him in front of the library."

"And?" Nina probed.

"And nothing." Amy lifted her other foot, studying her arch critically. If she focused on things re-
lated to dance, she wouldn't think about Sam.

"Not even a smile and hello between old friends?"
Dani asked. She and Nina had known Sam back in
high school, but no longer kept in touch. "Come on,
Amy. I know you both well enough to see through
that."

"My sentiments exactly," Nina said.

"All right. We greeted each other, but there
weren't any smiles. In fact, we almost broke into
an argument right there on the sidewalk. That's
about it." But even as Amy said the words, she recalled Sam's avid interest and suggestive comments. When he looked at her as if he were hungry
and she was the food he wanted, well… Her eyelids drifted closed. Her limbs felt languorous and
heavy, and for one long moment, she indulged in
the pleasure of remembering exactly how good a
lover he'd been.

"An argument, huh?" Dani chuckled. "Sounds just like old times."

Amy's eyes popped open. Good golly, fantasizing about Sam when she wasn't even interested. "For a minute it felt like old times, too. Then we decided to work at getting along, for Mariah's sake."

"That sounds wise and very mature," Nina said.

"That's me, Miss Mature." This time Amy's sigh was loud enough that both her friends heard it.

"Where did *that* sad sound come from?" Dani's voice resonated with concern.

Amy had no secrets from her two best friends. She reached for her loofah sponge and a bar of handmade glycerin soap. "The truth is, I'm envious of you both." She scrubbed one arm, then the other, then rinsed beneath the water. "I'd like to fall in love, get married and have a baby. I'm nearly thirty, and if my reproductive system's anything like my mother's, time is running out."

Her mother had tried for ages to conceive. After eight years, at the age of thirty-seven, she'd at last become pregnant with Amy. Much to everyone's regret, her parents were unable to give her siblings. Amy worried that she could have the same problems getting pregnant. As soon as the recital was over and her school closed for the summer, she intended to mount a full-scale search for a husband. He had to want kids right away, and he had to understand about the importance of dance in her life.

"Given that you're well into Saturn return, that's understandable," Nina said. "You're ready to get serious about the rest of your life. And with your being a Taurus and ruled by Venus, that means love and marriage. It's going to happen," she finished with certainty.

Amy didn't put much faith in astrology, but she grasped on to her friend's words like a beacon of hope. Pathetic as that was. She sighed again. "Too bad there aren't any men around to get serious with."

"Of course there are," Dani assured her. "Who knows, the man of your dreams could be right in front of you, only you don't know it."

An excited gasp issued from Nina, which meant she'd just had an "aha" insight. "Hey, what about Sam? Now that you're both full-fledged adults—"

"Absolutely not." Abruptly Amy sat up. Water sloshed over the sides of the tub and onto the blue-and-white tile floor. She frowned as her matching blue-and-white hand-hooked oval rug rapidly absorbed the water. Darn it, she'd just laundered it.

Her mood darkened like the rug as she recalled the defiant jut of Sam's chin and the things she'd heard about him over the years. He'd been paired with a number of women, but nothing had lasted. He seemed to grow tired of his girlfriends—or maybe they refused to let him run their lives. Amy knew the routine well. Sam had expected her to take care of him and their home, never mind her own career. As for babies, no thank you. He wanted all the attention fixed on him. No doubt he was still as domineering as ever.

She frowned. "Sam hasn't changed a bit. No, it has to be a man who's not afraid to share his thoughts, and who respects my career and dreams as much as I respect his. A man who believes I'm his equal and who treats me that way. Someone who won't hurt me by putting his needs first and ignoring mine." She located the loofah in the tub and re-lathered it.

"At least she knows what she wants," Nina commented drily.

"Which is good." Dani's knitting needles clicked and clacked furiously. "You need a game plan. Hmm… You've always given one hundred percent to dance. Maybe you should look at finding the right man the same way, as an all-out effort and a full-time job. What do you think, Nina?"

"I think that's a great idea. Don't you, Amy?"

Amy lifted her leg. "It's worth a try. I'll give it my all, just as soon as I get through this recital," she promised as she scrubbed her calf with long, clean strokes.

"Your special guy's out there, I know it. Your astrological chart indicates it, and the stars don't lie."

So, okay, astrology wasn't Amy's thing. Still, you never knew. Optimism unfurled in her chest. "I hope you're right."

"YOU VOLUNTEERED ME FOR *WHAT?*" Sam shot his niece a look of disbelief as he eased the Porsche into the dance studio's rain-slicked parking lot Friday afternoon. Traffic had been light, and they were early.

"To help make the sets we need for the recital."

Sam groaned as he shut off the wipers and then the ignition. "Why'd you do that?"

Mariah scrunched down in her seat with a guilty look, accompanied by raindrops pounding the car's windshield and roof. "Because everybody's parents volunteer. Mom and Dad aren't around, and I thought…" She bit her lip and hugged her gym bag. "Are you mad at me?"

Sam hated the way her slender shoulders bowed while she studied her lap, as if all the problems in the world weighed her down. Guilt pricked him. The last thing he wanted was to make the kid feel bad. "Nah. I just wish you'd asked me first."

When Mariah blew out a loud, relieved breath, he knew he'd said the right thing. She unbuckled her seat belt and turned toward him. "I know I should have talked to you about it first, Uncle Sam, but we really need you. We're doing the dance of the elves and fairies, and somebody has to build the magic forest."

"Somebody, huh?"

She fixed him with the impish, big-eyed look

that had wrapped him around her little finger from the moment of her birth. He couldn't help chuckling. "Just when am I supposed to find the time to help with the sets?"

"Maybe on weekends, when you don't work. But you should check with Miss Parker."

"And where are you supposed to be while I'm doing this volunteer work?" he asked, still smarting from Amy's comments last night. She'd practically accused him of child neglect. "I can't exactly leave you by yourself."

"I can go to a friend's house, or we can get Claudia to baby-sit. She loves taking care of me."

The sixteen-year-old sitter lived a block down from Mariah. Sam had met her, and he trusted her. He nodded. "We'll see."

That seemed enough of a promise for Mariah. "Come on, Uncle Sam." She pushed open her door, calling over her shoulder as she hopped out. "It'll be fun."

"A real party," he muttered. Just what he wanted to do, volunteer for Amy. The woman had haunted his dreams last night, and if it had been up to him, he'd have stayed away. Dreading the prospect of seeing Amy again, he stepped out of the car and watched his niece skip happily around puddles and through the rain toward the door.

Mariah's parents had been gone three days, but it felt like forever. Still, he owed it to the girl to make the next two and a half weeks enjoyable. What was the big deal, anyway? Last night he and Amy had agreed to be civil to each other. They even shook hands on it.

Sam thought about the feel of her palm in his, and his blood stirred. He snorted with self-disgust. There was nothing between them but history and old memories, some damn painful. Rain pelted him, so he sprinted toward the shelter of the eaves where Mariah awaited him.

With the back of his hand he swiped the moisture from his face, then opened the door. "Let's get this over with."

Mariah darted through the door. Feeling like a cowboy heading for a shoot-out, he sucked in a breath and followed her inside.

Unlike the other day, today the stage was empty. Amy stood at the barre, along with a group of older kids—Rubies, Sam knew. They were middle schoolers, and their school day started and ended before Mariah's. Likewise, their rehearsal started and finished each day before the Pearls'.

Mariah hung back, her head tilted as she scrutinized the dancers. Sam stayed beside her. He could see both Amy and her reflection, and the double images made quite a picture. Today she wore a V-neck black leotard, a tiny, pink wraparound skirt and pink tights. The outfit hugged her every curve, showing off her lithe waist, slender hips and shapely behind as she bent and then gracefully straightened. Her small, round breasts lifted as she raised her arms and drew in a breath.

Sam remembered the warm, soft feel of her in his arms as if he'd held her yesterday. Desire blind-sided him, along with the urge to touch her. His fingers curled at his sides.

"Leg up, and twirl," she directed in a soft, yet commanding voice. Boys and girls positioned their feet and arms, and Amy moved with them. Holding her posture ramrod-straight, she called out various movements while demonstrating by shifting her legs, feet, arms and hands. Sam remembered enough to know that she was working them through their steps.

Despite disagreements and heated arguments about her career, he'd always enjoyed watching her dance. But after so many years away, her fluid grace captivated him. "Beautiful," he murmured softly.

His niece shot him a curious look. "What did you say?"

He had to think fast. He gestured to the pink slippers on Amy's feet. "She's not wearing toe shoes," he said.

"That's because none of us are old enough to dance en pointe."

"Ah."

"You boys know what to do," Amy said. "I'd like you to watch as I perform the girls' part, because despite two full weeks of rehearsals, none of you has got it quite right yet." The kids left the barre and gathered around her, leaving room for her to dance. Their faces were alight with interest, and so was Amy's. "Watch me," she said, rising slightly on her toes. "Adagio, and pirouette."

Sam caught his breath as she demonstrated the simple, graceful twirl. She repeated the steps, explaining the moves. When she finished she leaned down, her hand sweeping just above the floor as she executed a ballet curtsy. Admiration filled Sam. He couldn't help clapping.

Amy swiveled her head his way. "Oh," she said, and even from a distance of thirty feet, he noted the flush staining her cheeks. His own face warmed and he wished he'd kept quiet. He shoved his hands into his pockets. At the same time, her hand fluttered to her neatly corralled hair, smoothing it back.

Boys and girls turned toward him, curiosity etched on their faces.

He shifted uncomfortably. "Mariah says you need a volunteer to help with the sets."

"Yes, I do," Amy said, looking both surprised and disconcerted. "Can you wait ten minutes? We'll be finished then."

She moved to the CD player. The music started, the same piece he'd heard the other day. The young females attempted the steps, their male partners holding on to their waists. There were more girls than boys, and several girls paired up.

Almost lovingly and with great patience, Amy walked slowly among them, calling out instructions over the music. Often she offered encouragement or stopped to help position a dancer's arm or leg. By the happy expression on her face and her patient ministrations, he knew she genuinely enjoyed working with these kids. Not only that, she didn't seem to mind that they weren't very good. She wasn't the do-it-right-or-die-trying perfectionist Sam remembered. At least not at the moment.

His eyes on Amy, he heard the door open. "Here comes Janelle Swanson and her mom," Mariah said in a low voice.

Sam glanced over his shoulder in time to see a petite, blonde woman and a girl Mariah's age saunter in. "It's Mrs. Swanson's turn to bring snacks and help out," Mariah explained. "See you later, Uncle Sam."

She ran to meet Janelle. Heads bent together and whispering, the girls walked off together, leaving Sam alone with the blonde. She was about his age, with a carefully made-up face. Her hair was cut in a sophisticated style, and her silk slacks and blouse exactly matched her suede pumps. A large, solitaire diamond glinted in the hollow of her tanned throat. In that outfit, she would have fit in well at a country club luncheon.

"I'm Connie Swanson," she smiled, smoothing

her hands down her hips. A flashy, ruby-studded tennis bracelet decorated her wrist. She eyed Sam with blatant interest. "Who are *you*?"

"Sam Cutter, Amy's uncle," he said, ignoring the suggestive innuendo in her tone. He did not mess with married women, but even if she were single, she didn't interest him. Which was surprising, considering she was exactly the type he'd dated for years—rich and attractive.

"*The* Sam Cutter?" Connie's eyes widened. "Wow. My ex-husband is a great admirer of yours. What you've accomplished with your fast-food restaurant chain is nothing short of amazing."

"Thanks." So she was divorced. Not that that changed things. Sam still wasn't interested.

She added, "I've been divorced for three years, but Bob and I are still friends. He's a partner in an investment firm in town. Swanson and Davis?"

That explained the jewelry and expensive clothes. No doubt the ex paid out hefty alimony and child support. Sam nodded. "I've heard of them."

He turned his attention to the front of the room. Amy and the group had moved onstage, where they were now working on the steps they'd just practiced. Their legs were out of sync, but they wore confident expressions. Thanks to Amy.

"Say, Sam," Connie murmured in a low voice. She moved closer, and he caught a whiff of her perfume, something pricey. He didn't care for the scent—too strong and too sweet. She cupped his biceps and leaned in close. "I'd love to get together and discuss your work sometime."

If ever Sam had heard a come-on, this was it. Making no secret of his feelings, he narrowed his eyes as he lifted her manicured hand from his arm and put some distance between them. "Taking care of Mariah and running the business uses up all my time. Since I'll be working on the sets, I'm even busier."

"Well now, isn't that a lovely coincidence?" A provocative smile lit the blonde's face. "I'll be working on those sets, too."

Wonderful. Sam scowled and searched out his niece. At that moment, the music stopped and Amy dismissed the group.

"Nice work, Rubies," she said, beaming. "See you tomorrow morning at nine."

Thank you, Amy. Glad to get away from man-hungry Connie, Sam strode toward the stage. Amy saw him coming. Her smile vanished. Hands on her hips, her expression cool, she didn't exactly look pleased that he'd been volunteered. He wasn't thrilled, either, but he preferred her displeasure to Connie's blatant flirtation.

Wait a minute. A cute, sexy blonde stood at the back of the room, practically salivating over him, and he'd rather talk to his frowning ex-wife, whom he'd hoped never to see for the rest of his life?

He'd definitely lost his mind.

Chapter Three

SHORTLY AFTER NOON on Saturday, the door clicked shut behind the last of Amy's students and a peaceful silence filled the studio. Usually Amy cherished the sudden stillness, a welcome relief after a busy session of nonstop noise and activity. Not today. She cast a black look at the closed door of the storage room behind the stage, where Sam and Connie were working on the sets for the upcoming recital. They were awfully quiet in there.

Resisting the urge to climb the steps, stalk across the stage and eavesdrop at the door, Amy instead tugged off her ballet slippers. Then, arching forward, she massaged the small of her back. Normally the school was closed weekends, but with the recital only a month away and the kids in need of extra practice time, she had opened today until noon.

Thank goodness there were no more classes until Monday, because after this morning's three-plus hours of the hustle and bustle and continuous demands on her attention, she was worn out. Yet she was also oddly restless and edgy. But then, with Sam and Connie here…well, the very air seemed charged with tension.

The muscle in her hip ached, and she pressed her knuckles into it as she walked toward the coat closet beyond the mirrored wall, her stocking feet whispering over the polished wood floor and her mind on the man and woman behind the storage room door.

Connie had arrived first, in time to deliver her daughter Janelle to the Pearls' hour-long rehearsal. Afterward, Sam had shown up and Mariah had left with Jessica Stevens. Janelle went home with Delia Jeffries. Her mother stayed behind to work on the sets. Dressed in tight, faded jeans and a low-neck, form-hugging T-shirt, the blonde no doubt planned to work on Sam, too.

The woman was a flirt. Amy frowned as she flung open the closet, took her grass-green corduroy overalls from the hook and stepped into them. She pulled her braid free, then fastened the straps of her overalls over her leotard. Retrieving her clogs, she toed into them. A quick glance at her reflection shocked her. Her mouth was pinched sourly and her brow furrowed. Muttering, she smoothed her expression. If Connie wanted to flirt and more, that was of no concern to Amy. None whatsoever.

Sam certainly didn't appear to mind. True, yesterday he'd seemed on edge, almost panicky about teaming up with Connie. But today he'd seemed eager enough. Maybe he liked the idea of working alone in the back room with the buxom blonde. What man wouldn't?

As if to reinforce Amy's thoughts, muted female laughter sounded through the storage room door. Exactly what kind of work were they doing in there? Amy snatched her canvas duffel from the closet shelf, then shut the door with more force than necessary.

From out of nowhere, jealousy whacked her hard, smack in the middle of her chest. Duffel in hand she stalked back to the bench, aggravating her stressed hip muscle. She winced, but not entirely from the pain. Jealous of Connie and Sam? Now that was absolutely ridiculous. She shoved her slippers into the bag.

How could she possibly be jealous when she didn't care a whit about Sam Cutter?

Her stomach growled, which explained that hollow feeling inside. Of course. She was hungry and her hip hurt. She should get some air, walk out the kinks and grab lunch.

She glanced again at the storage room, wondering whether to tell Sam and Connie she was leaving. Not that they'd care. Still, they ought to know. She climbed the steps to the stage and headed toward the work area. When she was nearly there, Connie squealed.

Enough already. Amy rolled her eyes. Suddenly the door flew open and Sam strode out, his jaw clamped, his face dark and his attention on the wooden floor. He plowed smack into Amy.

She tried to moved aside, stumbling in her haste. Reaching out, she caught a handful of his navy T-shirt to steady herself.

"Whoa, there." Sam cupped her elbows and eyed her curiously.

Her cheeks heated as she slipped from his grasp. "Thanks." Meeting his gaze made her uncomfortable, maybe because only seconds ago he'd been laughing with Connie, so she frowned at the fist-sized wrinkles she'd put on his shirt.

"Sorry." Of their own volition her palms smoothed the soft cotton, skimming Sam's chest. His firm, very broad chest. Under her palms his heart thudded. Amy's heart thudded, too, so hard that surely he heard. She swallowed and lifted her hands. Or tried.

He stopped her, trapping her wrists against his heart. Warmth from his fingers penetrated the fabric of her long-sleeve leotard. Hunger simmered in his eyes, turning them a darker blue as he searched her face.

"Amy," he murmured in a husky tone that bathed her in warmth. It was only her name, but from his lips it sounded important and special.

With his hands on her wrists she could not move,

nor did she attempt to. Standing so close, she could smell him, the mixture of pine soap and man achingly familiar, even after twelve years. Her senses stirred with the memory, and longing rushed over her, so intense, she yearned to wrap her arms around his waist and sink against him. That scared her witless. She narrowed her eyes. "Let go, Sam."

He did, reeling as if his heated reaction had caught him off guard as well. Quick as a heartbeat, he banked his expression, folded his arms over his chest and fixed her with a now-impenetrable gaze. Except when he desired her, he'd never been easy to read, but the sudden slant of his brows and the downward curl of his lips told her plenty. He might want her, but he didn't like it. Feeling the same way, she completely understood.

"You okay?" he asked, his gruff tone matching his expression.

"Fine," she lied, sounding breathless to her own ears. "You're in an awful hurry. What's the rush?"

He glanced behind him at the closed storeroom door, then leaned in as if to confide a secret. "Connie thinks I'm heading out to pick up lunch," he said in a low voice. "And I am, but I want to talk with you first."

After what had just happened she'd have preferred that Sam leave now. But this seemed important. So she nodded and did what she always did when nervous, reached for her braid and flipped it over her shoulder. "What is it?"

His gaze dropped to the loose end of her braid, which hung to just below her breast. Raw emotion flickered in his eyes, then disappeared before she could figure out what it meant.

He cleared his throat and pulled his attention to her face. "Uh, I could use your help."

The man had never asked her for help. Never. She couldn't stem her surprise. "Oh?"

"It's Connie." He shot a second harried look over his shoulder. "She's driving me nuts."

For a moment Amy was speechless. Then she threw him a skeptical look. "Puh-leeze. I'm not deaf. You two have been laughing since you walked in there and closed the door."

"Connie did all the laughing. I swear, I haven't cracked a smile yet. I've done everything short of telling her to get lost, but she can't seem to understand that I'm not interested. I don't know how to handle her."

As Amy thought about it, she realized she hadn't heard masculine laughter. Maybe Sam didn't like the sexy flirt, after all. The knowledge loosened the cold knot in her chest. "She can come on pretty strong," she agreed.

"Like a barracuda." Sam grimaced. "I promised Mariah I'd help with the sets, and I want to keep my word." His expression glum, he shook his head. "But I won't stay in a room alone with that woman."

Now there was a dilemma Amy had not anticipated. "But Connie's one of my best volunteers, and the only person besides you who offered help with the sets. I'd hate to lose her, and I know you don't want to be stuck doing all the work by yourself."

"Since I don't have the time, you got that right. Are you sure there's no one else you can recruit? Some kid's dad?"

Amy shook her head. "Believe me, I've tried everyone. The parents who can help are working on other parts of the recital."

"Well then, we have a problem." Sam rocked back on his heels and rubbed his chin thoughtfully. Suddenly his gaze homed in on Amy. "You could join us."

Work alongside Sam and Connie in the back room? Amy spoke her mind. "That's an interesting idea, except for one big hitch. You and I can barely tolerate each other." Even standing here on the open stage with him was difficult.

Her remark earned her a quick, inscrutable look. "True," he readily agreed. "But can you think of any other solution?" He shrugged. "Either you want my help, or you don't."

Like it or not she couldn't afford to lose him. "I want it," she said with reluctance.

"Then I need a chaperone."

She fiddled with her braid while she considered her options. Short of tackling the sets herself or asking Connie to finish up alone, there were none. She gave in with a grudging sigh. "I do have plans later on today, but for the sake of the recital, I suppose I could stay and help for a while."

Sam let out a relieved breath. "Thank you."

A sudden idea struck her, and she held up a finger. "But there is something I'd like in return."

"Besides making the sets?" He shot her a guarded look.

"If you wouldn't mind. During the recital, I need an adult backstage to take care of last-minute details. I don't allow parents to help because they should be out front, enjoying the program."

Sam nodded. "Sure, I could do that." Amy's stomach gurgled loudly. His brows raised a fraction. "Sounds like you need to eat. I'm headed to Cutter's to pick up lunch. Do you still like veggie burgers?"

"I sure do."

As Sam headed out the door, she told herself she dreaded this afternoon. Yet already she anticipated his return. She caught herself and frowned. Where in the world was her common sense? She had no interest in Sam. Once was enough, and besides, only a fool would make the same mistake twice.

And Amy was no fool.

FORTY-FIVE MINUTES later the aroma of hamburgers, onion rings and fries filled the studio. Sam leaned forward in his folding chair near the stage and lobbed his napkin into the large, now-empty lunch sack he'd brought from Cutter's. He was the first to finish, though Connie and Amy, who sat in identical chairs opposite him, were nearly through.

Fusion jazz played softly from the radio station Amy had chosen, and her foot tapped the floor in time to the beat. He still couldn't believe he'd asked her to stick around, or that she'd agreed to stay. But he'd needed a buffer between him and Connie. With Amy desperate for someone to build the sets in time for the upcoming recital, her help in return for his seemed a fair trade.

He glanced warily at Connie, who had finished her lunch. For the moment she was quiet with concentration, hunched over a small hand mirror to apply a fresh coat of rose-red lipstick.

So different from Amy. In the past, she'd never used lipstick except on rare occasions. From what Sam had observed, that hadn't changed. Ditching his straw, he drained the last of his Italian soda.

Connie mooshed her lips together in the universal facial gesture women made after applying lipstick. Seemingly unconcerned about primping in front of him, she dug into her purse for a comb and then ran it through her hair. The ultra-blond color probably came from a bottle. Amy's hair color was a natural light brown. She wore it long and pulled back like a dancer, the same as years ago. Oddly, the style still suited her. A few loose strands fluttered softly around her face. One longer, thick lock brushed the corner of her eye. She kept pushing that one back, but the stubborn thing wouldn't stay put. Sam wished she'd find a hair clip and anchor it behind her ear. If he had one, he'd do it himself. Was her hair as soft as he remembered? He itched to find out. Frowning, he rolled his empty bottle between his palms.

He wasn't interested in Amy. Clearly she wasn't interested in him, either. Other than when he'd returned with lunch, she'd barely glanced at him.

Connie dropped her tools into her purse and smiled. "That was delicious, Sam," she cooed, clasping her hands beneath her chin and lowering her mascara-laden lashes. "You are a sweetheart."

On the other hand, the artificial blonde had continued to flirt shamelessly. Sam rolled his eyes at the tile ceiling.

"It *was* good," Amy agreed, wiping her hands on a napkin. "Thank you, Sam." She folded her veggie burger wrapper into a small square, then did the same with her napkin. She'd always been like that, neat and tidy.

"You're both welcome." He stood. "Ready to get back to work?" He held out the paper sack, collecting trash.

Connie and Amy led the way up the stage stairs and across the stage to the storage room, while he lagged behind. Even their walks were different.

Connie moved in a hip-swaying step, her skintight jeans accentuating her small waist and shapely rear end. No red-blooded man could fail to notice, including Sam. But he felt nothing beyond mild interest. It was Amy's loose overalls and clean, no-nonsense stride that quickened his blood. And that darkened his mood. Dammit, he was here to work, not desire a woman he couldn't have—and didn't want.

Scowling, he followed the women through the door. The fluorescent lighting that filled the windowless room with harsh light did nothing to brighten his mood.

"Take a look at the trees we started this morning," he told Amy. Skirting props, bolts of fabric and various odds and ends, he reached the ceiling-high shelves that lined one wall. A half dozen six-foot-high plywood trees, each painted dark brown, leaned against the shelves. "There's another one over there." He gestured toward the back of the windowless room, where a horizontal tree was balanced on two sawhorses. "Now that the paint is dry, they're ready for leaves."

"Which I traced and started cutting out while Sam made the trees." Connie pointed to the squares of green felt and the two-inch cutouts piled on the cluttered counter. "I have a ton more to cut."

"I'm impressed with the level of detail," Amy said with a pleased smile. "The kids will love this.

As fairies and elves, they'll dance happily in your enchanted forest."

"That's what Mariah said." His niece had driven him crazy repeating the story that framed each dance, which Amy and the entire group had developed together. His mouth quirked. "Once we glue on the leaves, we'll add glitter, some of that spider webbing people use for Halloween, and a lot of strategically placed dry ice to turn our forest into the magical place it becomes at midnight."

"Sam can get the dry ice through Cutter's," Connie added. "And I have a big, round moon I bought once for a party. I thought I'd spray paint it silver and then dust it with glitter. I'll also sew a chiffon curtain to hang across the stage for atmosphere, and glittery clouds to go with the moon."

"What great ideas," Amy said with sincerity. "But those things are going to take time." Head tilted she threw Sam a questioning look he easily interpreted— could he handle working again with Connie? "Are you sure you're willing to put in that much effort?"

The blonde nodded. "Things move fast when Sam and I work together. We make a fantastic team." In the artificial light, her lipstick looked garish and unflattering, and her cheeks unnaturally pink from a makeup overdose. She arched one brow suggestively and waved her long, rose-painted nails in a dismissive gesture. "I know you're busy, Amy. There's really no need for you to stay and help."

Sam didn't hide his disagreement, frowning as he slanted his hip against the door. "I want Amy here."

Only to act as a buffer, he told himself.

Connie's mouth tightened, and she looked ready to argue. Dreading a debate, and not wanting to explain, he sent Amy a silent, urgent appeal he hoped she wouldn't refuse. So far she'd played her part well.

Her eyes widened a fraction, and then she dipped her head in a subtle nod of understanding. "I'm not planning to take over or anything. I just figured since both of you have limited time, and I have a few hours free this afternoon, an extra pair of hands would speed things along."

"I see." Connie nodded, but her gaze narrowed appraisingly as she looked from Sam to Amy. "I'd heard you two were once married to each other. But I never realized… Sometimes I am so thick-headed! You're getting together again, aren't you?"

The very words made Sam cringe. The last thing he wanted was to start up something with Amy. "There's not a chance in hell of that," he stated, while Amy reinforced the sentiment with a vigorous shake of her head.

Connie opened her mouth, no doubt to make matters worse. Thankfully, the sudden ring of a cell phone put an end to the conversation. "That's mine. Excuse me." She retrieved the slim phone from her purse and flipped it open. "Hello?" Adjusting her thick gold earring, she listened, then frowned, turned her back and lowered her voice. A moment later she hung up. "That was Janelle. She's not feeling well and wants me to come get her. One of her friends had strep last week. I just hope Janelle hasn't contracted it. If it is strep, you may want to run Mariah to the doctor, Sam, and get her started on medicine. In any case, I'm afraid I'll have to leave."

"I'm so sorry," Amy said. "Tell Janelle I hope she feels better soon."

Though Sam wasn't sorry to see the blonde go, he managed a nod of agreement.

"We'll have to schedule another work party later." Waving her fingers, Connie sashayed toward the door. "You two have fun. I'll call you to arrange a time, Sam."

"I wish you wouldn't," he muttered, but she didn't seem to hear. As her mules clicked loudly across the wood stage, he frowned at Amy. "No wonder that woman is divorced. Her husband should have put a stop to her outrageous behavior long ago."

Instead of a nod of agreement, his words earned him a scathing look. "I admit, I don't care for her flirtatious ways, and I'm sure her ex-husband didn't, either. But Connie is the sole person responsible for her actions, not her ex-husband or anyone else."

Having no clue what she meant, Sam angled her a puzzled look.

"You don't get it, do you? But why is that a surprise?" Amy sighed and shot him an imperious frown. "Not all men keep their women on the short rein you do."

Both her voice and the you-are-so-clueless look irritated Sam. Hanging his thumbs from the belt loops of his jeans, he narrowed his eyes. "What in hell are you talking about?"

"Don't you remember?" Anger flashed in her eyes as she lifted her chin. "You wanted to be the boss, run the house and control me."

"Control you," he repeated, shaking his head at the long fluorescent bulbs hanging overhead. "All I wanted was for us to have the kind of marriage my parents had." Back then, he'd believed his father's tight handle on the family and household had been the glue that solidified his parents' relationship. He'd learned the sad truth sometime later, after his divorce—and theirs. "If that bothered you, you never said so."

"I know. I was young and confused. We both were." Absently fingering the tiny silver hoop in her earlobe, Amy stared glumly into space, as if their failed marriage lay in tatters before her. With a sigh, she turned her attention to him, offering a thin smile. "But it doesn't matter anymore."

It mattered, a lot more than Sam cared to admit. "It does when you still resent me."

Amy bit her lip and glanced at the littered floor.

Needing to see her eyes, Sam closed the gap between them and tipped up her chin. Her skin was soft and warm against his hand, and he caught the faint scent of vanilla. That was something new that he definitely liked.

A parade of emotions rolled across Amy's face. Surprise, then anger, then hurt. She'd always been as easy to see through as a picture window.

She jerked her head from his grasp, backing away until the scarred counter lining the wall stopped her. "I quit resenting you a long time ago."

"Did you?" he snorted in disbelief. "Well, I still resent you."

Her eyes widened. "Why, for defying your need to control me?"

"For walking out." And for the months of pain, misery and loneliness that followed.

"One of us had to leave," she said. "We agreed on that." She shook her head sadly. "It was the only thing we ever agreed on."

Sam conceded the point with a nod. "Except for when to make love. We were in perfect harmony there."

Her mouth curled in a smirk. "It always comes back to sex, doesn't it? Physical attraction is the only thing we ever had, Sam. And when that no longer was enough…" Regret shadowed her eyes, and the words trailed off. Her gaze darted away from his. She picked a felt leaf from the small mountain of green on the counter, smoothing her fingers over it.

Unfortunately, Sam had never lost his desire for Amy. For years, he'd dreamed about her. He'd badly wanted her the other day when Mariah had first dragged him into the studio. And the night in front of the library. And today, before lunch. With her braid slung over her shoulder, her cheeks flushed and her lower lip caught between her teeth, he wanted her again, now. Hell, he wanted her all the time. But he'd never admit it, and he sure wasn't going to act on his desire. He was not going to kiss her, or anything else. Period.

He scrubbed his hand over his face. "Look, I don't want to rehash what went wrong between us."

"I don't, either," Amy replied, her mouth turned into a hopeless frown. She released a heavy sigh. "I want us to get along."

"All right, then." He grabbed the glue gun from the counter and pointed it toward the sawhorse. "How about helping me put the leaves on these trees?"

Chapter Four

WHEN AMY'S WATCH alarm beeped two hours later, she was amazed. Placing leaves so they looked right required an incredible amount of concentration and effort. For that reason, the long, uncomfortably tense afternoon she'd anticipated had flown by. She'd actually laughed some, too. Which was remarkable, considering she'd done her laughing with Sam.

She tacked two leaves onto a now-verdant tree branch before silencing the alarm. "Looks like it's time for me to go."

Sam flipped the switch on the glue gun. "Too bad." He clapped his mouth shut as if he hadn't meant to say that, then set aside the gun and cleared his throat. "What I mean is, we're on a roll here. Look how much we finished."

Amy glanced at the two leaf-laden trees balanced against the cabinet. "We must have cut and glued several hundred leaves." Within fifteen minutes they'd run through the pile Connie had cut.

"You gotta admit, that's impressive. Once we set aside our differences and got down to business, we did okay."

She nodded. "Proving that people can accomplish anything if they work hard enough."

"Why didn't we work this hard when we were married?" His eyes searched her face in genuine puzzlement.

Equally mystified, Amy shook her head. "I don't know. I guess we were too young to know how."

"Probably."

At that, both went silent, lost in their own private thoughts. When Amy glanced at Sam a moment later, he was staring at her. As their glances collided the easy familiarity between them shifted into something far less relaxed. Awareness. Suddenly the very air between them vibrated with it. Sam's expression warmed, and his eyes turned smoky and intense and smoldering. Amy went all hot inside. The blood throbbed in her ears, and every nerve in her body stood poised and waiting for his attention.

Not again. She stepped behind a tree stretched across two sawhorses, using it as a barrier between her and Sam. "I really do have to go."

"Hot date?" he asked, his expression inscrutable.

"No."

Was that relief on his face? "What then?" he asked.

"Remember Nina Bartlett?" Amy waited for his nod, then continued. "She's getting married."

"Send her my sympathies," he quipped.

His gaze lost its intensity and his mouth stretched in a semigrin. The tension between them eased, and things seemed more comfortable and lighthearted. Amy could breathe easy again.

"I'm not going to tell her that." Feigning irritation, she planted her hands on her hips and offered her own smirk. "I'll give her your congratulations and best wishes." When Sam frowned, she smiled. "Anyway, Dani and I are getting together tonight to plan the bachelorette party."

"Dani, huh? From what I remember, when the three of you get together…" Sam shook his head knowingly. "That's going to be some wild party."

"Not this time. Dani's pregnant with twins, and that's bound to temper the evening."

"Two babies? Whoa. I'm having trouble with one eight-year-old."

He looked so appalled that Amy laughed. "Dani and Russ are really excited. They've put away quite a bit of money, so they'll be able to hire help if they need it."

"They'll need all the help they can get, I guarantee it. Congratulate her for me, will you?"

"Sure." That pesky lock of hair brushed the corner of Amy's eye. She blew it off her face, but it quickly dropped back.

Sam frowned and moved around the tree, until he stood inches from her. "I can't stand this anymore."

He tucked the lock behind her ear, his jaw flexed in concentration and his touch awkward. When the strands sprang loose again, he shook his head. "Don't you have something to keep that out of your eyes?"

"I lost my hair clip."

"Then get another."

"Yes, sir."

They reached for the offending lock at the same time. Their fingers collided. Electricity jolted between them, too strong to ignore. Amy snapped her hand away, but Sam's stayed put.

"Damn stubborn thing." His expression sobered as he smoothed his palm over her hair.

He touched her temple and the sensitive crest of her ear, and her mind clouded. "Me, or my hair?"

"Both."

Those sensual fingers continued their caress while his hot gaze held her. Amy told herself to back away. Instead, she leaned into his touch. "You're not exactly flexible yourself," she murmured.

His mouth quirked, while his hand stilled above her ear. "At the moment, a certain part of my anatomy is anything but."

She managed a disapproving look even as her pulse rate kicked up another notch. "We're back to sex again."

"Can't seem to get away from it, can we?" Sam's

eyes darkened with a need that matched the ache inside her. "We definitely have a problem," he said in a voice as rich as liquid smoke. "We're going to have to deal with it sooner or later."

"Oh?" His fingers trailed to her cheek, making it difficult to think, let alone speak. "How so?"

Were his hands trembling, or was it her own shaky nerves? He inched closer. "We both have this need to find out whether we're as good together as we used to be."

That could be dangerous, she wanted to say. But with his breath warm on her face and his eyes bright and hot as molten silver, she could only nod.

Lifting his other hand, he cupped her face. "Just one kiss, and then we can put this misplaced attraction behind us."

Maybe he had a point. It would be very nice indeed to move past the unwanted desire that kept her awake at night and on edge by day. Besides, right now she *needed* to kiss him the way she needed to dance. "All right," she said on a breathy sigh. "But just one kiss."

"One," he agreed solemnly.

His hands slid to her shoulders and then to her waist. Her arms knew what to do, and natural as you please, she clasped the back of his neck. Her body tingled with familiar expectation, shaping to his as if she'd last kissed him yesterday.

She didn't wait for him to initiate contact. Stand-

ing on her toes, she rose up to meet him. His eyelids lowered to half-mast, then drifted shut. Released from the spell of his gaze, she panicked. *This
is a terrible mistake!*

Then his lips touched hers, and she was lost.

JUST ONE KISS, Sam reminded himself as Amy released a yielding sigh. Her hands tugged him down,
urging him closer, and her subtle vanilla scent
wrapped around him as tight and warm as her arms.
It had been a long time since he'd held her, and it
felt so damn good. In a wash of sensation and need,
he brushed his mouth over hers. She moved impa-
tiently and canted her head toward his, seeking more
than a light kiss. Dear God, she was sweet. A groan
slipped from his throat.

One kiss, he silently and firmly repeated. Then
she angled closer, her soft breasts against his chest
and her thighs flush with his, and his resolve crum-
bled. One more couldn't hurt. He stood a good half
foot taller than she and out of habit he lifted her for
easier access. She was light and supple and eager,
and suddenly it was if they'd never been apart. The
blood roared in his head and he coaxed her lips
open. This is crazy, he thought as he probed the
slick depths of her mouth with his tongue.

"Sam," she whispered in the throaty, hungry
voice he knew so well, even after all these years. She
pressed her hips against his pulsing groin. Desire

and need pounded through him, and he forgot to think.

He wanted her. Now. Cupping her soft, round behind, he backed toward the wall on rubbery legs. In his haste, he bumped the tree supported between the sawhorses. One end clattered to the floor. The jolt to the back of his thigh, coupled with the sharp noise, pierced the fog in his brain.

What in hell am I doing? As if she had read his thoughts, Amy jerked back, breaking their connection. Sam released her.

"What was that noise?" she asked, glancing around the room. Her face and neck were flushed, telltale signs of arousal.

Good or bad, right or wrong, she wanted him as much as he wanted her. He swallowed an unsteady breath. "The unpainted tree," he said hoarsely. At her dazed, blank look, he added, "We knocked it off the sawhorse."

"Oh."

She touched her mouth—red from his kisses— with the tips of her fingers. Damned if he didn't want to kiss her again. And more. He squelched that urge, pronto. He wasn't about to get involved with Amy, sexually or otherwise, not again. Once had been enough. He glanced down and snickered to himself. Tell that to his body.

She bent down and picked up the fallen tree. Sam moved to help her but she waved him off. He understood. They needed to stay far away from each other.

He pushed the sawhorses together. "About what happened… Well, it was a bad idea." Bad, but very hot.

"Certainly was," Amy hastily agreed as she returned the tree to its place on the sawhorse. "At least now, we're out of each other's system."

Sam didn't believe that for a second, and by the way she pulled her braid over her shoulder and nervously fiddled with the ends without meeting his eye, he knew she didn't, either.

"Thank God for that," he said with all the conviction he could summon.

She nodded, and an uncomfortable beat of silence ticked between them. She made a show of glancing at her watch. "I have to go, or Dani will kill me."

She started for the door, and Sam trailed after. "I don't mean to get married, ever again," he said.

In the threshold she stopped, spun around and threw him a puzzled look. "What does that have to do with anything?"

Her genuine confusion made him feel foolish, and he shoved his hands into his hip pockets. "Nothing, I guess. I just don't want you getting the wrong idea about what happened."

She gestured away the words. "I'm no longer the naive girl I once was, Sam, so you can stop worrying. Besides you're not the kind of man I want. Would you get the light switch?" she asked as she moved through the door.

She was looking for a male totally different from him. That made perfect sense, so Sam didn't like or understand the cold feeling her statement caused in his gut. He frowned as he shut off the lights, plunging the workroom into darkness. "Enlighten me, Amy. What exactly is your type?"

"Someone who shares my goals—getting married and, shortly following the wedding, starting a family," she replied as they moved across the stage.

"Huh." Their footsteps plodded across the wood planks for several seconds while Sam absorbed the information. "You've changed."

She eyed him. "How so?"

"Used to be, dance was your life. Period."

"You're wrong, Sam," she said as they headed for the exit. "Yes, it was important, but it never was my whole life."

Scoffing, he opened the door and gestured her out. "Could have fooled me. You ate, slept and breathed dance. I came in a distant second, and our marriage didn't even register." After twelve years, that still smarted. He shoved open the door and gestured her out.

Her jaw dropped, followed by a gasp of disbelief. "That's not true. It's not fair, either. But then, what would you know about that?"

He could feel his blood pressure climb. He didn't want to have a fight, so he clamped his jaw and counted to ten before speaking. "Look, it was a long time ago," he replied in what he thought was a reasonable tone. "It doesn't matter anymore."

Amy didn't seem to believe him. "Apparently it does. Why else would you keep dredging up the past?" She laughed without humor. "Too bad you remember it all wrong."

Want to or not, he couldn't ignore her accusation. "You're out in left field, Amy."

"Ha!" With an incensed huff she whisked past him, into the waning light, her braid swishing angrily down her back. "If you want to pass blame on our failed marriage, start with yourself. You wanted a maid, not a wife. You only cared about sex and your career, never about what I wanted." She lifted her head to queenly heights and fixed him with an I-dare-you-to-dispute-that frown.

His temper climbed to match the ire glittering in her eyes, and he gritted his teeth against the urge to yell. "Not quite," he said evenly.

He'd wanted a repeat of his own family, his mother obeying his father's every whim. He'd thought Amy wanted that, too. When she hadn't… He'd never been good at expressing himself and had vented his frustration the only way he'd known how, by picking a fight. He wasn't like that anymore.

Amy folded her arms across her chest. "Uh-huh."

That smug tilt of her lips taunted him like nothing else could, and he couldn't resist baiting her. "There you go again, jumping to conclusions."

"And how would I know that?" She tossed her head. "You never talked to me, and I'm no mind reader."

"I'm talking now," he shouted as he lost the battle for control.

"Well, I don't want to listen," she replied in an equally heated voice.

For a few tense seconds they tried to stare each other down, and it was just like the worst of old times. Sam's anger faded as quickly as it had risen, replaced with self-disgust. Dammit, he didn't get sucked into arguments like this anymore. Glancing at the pavement, he sucked in a breath, corralled his emotions and decided to joke his way out of this mess. "I sure am glad we straightened things out," he quipped.

Amy's mouth set as she tried to hold on to her anger, but he kept his expression easy. She must have realized he really wanted a truce. Her eyes widened in clear astonishment, as if she couldn't believe the argument was over. Given their history, who could blame her? At last, the tension eased from her face. "Very funny, Sam."

He nodded, and the very air seemed to lighten with relief. "I'd better get going. I promised Mariah I'd pick her up about now," he said.

"And I'm so late, Dani's probably ready to call the Missing Persons Bureau. Thanks again for your help today." She turned and hurried toward her car, which was at the opposite end of the parking lot.

Sam inhaled the cool, spring air and watched her drive off in her cute, yellow Bug. What a day. In just under eight hours, he'd fended off a sexy blonde, kissed Amy passionately and then argued with her about a past that was dead and buried. He must be insane, and he wasn't happy about his lack of control. At least he'd salvaged their fight with a joke.

But how had she managed to stir him up in the first place? Ambling toward his Porsche, he rubbed his chin and mulled over the question. There was no explanation, and he was confused and worn out. What he needed was male camaraderie and a nice, cold beer. Thankfully his best buddies, Gabe and Josh, were coming over for pizza tonight. Gabe's wife and two preschoolers were out of town visiting her parents, and Josh's wife had to work, so the men had set up a get-together. Mariah adored them both. Good-natured guys, they'd agreed to watch a movie with Sam and her. They'd help put the frustrating day in perspective.

Just thinking about the relaxing evening ahead made him feel better, and he unlocked his car in lighter spirits. In no time at all, he'd forget about Amy and be back to his usual happy self.

Chapter Five

STILL REELING FROM a day filled with surprises, Amy checked for traffic on her way out of the parking lot. No cars, so she pulled out. So much had happened today, none of it planned, not even in her wildest imagination. She'd kissed Sam, argued with him and dredged up things that should have been laid to rest years ago. Now she was confused, an emotional wreck. She glanced at her watch. Yes, she was due at Dani's, but first she needed a moment to sort out her feelings. A block and a half down the street, she slipped into a parking space under a flowering magnolia tree and shut off the engine.

In the rearview mirror she watched Sam's sleek Porsche speed off in the opposite direction. The dark, sexy car fit him perfectly. Sometimes when he looked at her, his eyes had a way of lighting up and softening that made her go all mushy inside. Through high school and their marriage, she'd never been able to resist that look. Apparently she still couldn't. Wrapped in warmth, she sighed dreamily. He kissed even better than she remembered, his mouth gentle and teasing before he turned serious. And then, whoo-boy. Just remembering caused her heart to give a funny little kick and her insides to melt. She'd not only kissed Sam, she'd liked it. A lot. And that was bad, very bad.

Groaning, she buried her face in her hands. "Big mistake, Amy," she muttered. One of many today.

The sudden knock on her window startled her. She jerked up to see Kari Jeffries peering anxiously at her. "Are you all right?".

Amy cringed. The gossipy mom, whose daughter Delia was a Pearl and a good friend of Mariah's, was the last person she wanted to see. Forcing a smile, she rolled down her window. "I'm fine. What are you doing here?"

"It's such a nice afternoon, I thought I'd walk to the drugstore." She gestured to the one-story brick-and-wood structure a few yards down. "Delia's at home with her dad, puttering in the garden."

"She danced beautifully this morning," Amy said.

Kari smiled. "She told me." She cast a curious, yet knowing look at Amy. "My gosh, are you just now leaving the studio?"

The smug arch of her brow put Amy on alert. Had Kari walked past the studio in time to hear the exchange between her and Sam? Amy hoped not because if she had, in no time the woman would spread her version of things everywhere. Or maybe she was simply probing for information.

There was nothing to do but play along. "With the recital in a few weeks, there's still so much to do."

Delia's mother gave a small nod. As in, *go on.*

"Unfortunately, now I have a headache and need to buy some pain reliever," Amy prevaricated. Because of her hip she always carried a full bottle in her purse.

"I understand completely," Kari said with a cryptic smile. "Stress can cause all sorts of problems, including headaches and a short fuse." She winked. "A delicious man like Sam Cutter would definitely raise my stress level."

Dear me, she *did* know. Amy stiffened. "There's nothing between Sam and me," she said with a pointed look. "It's all in the past."

"Sure it is, honey." The woman looked as if she'd just heard the story of the year. "Connie Swanson phoned a while ago and told me all about it."

"Connie called you?" Amy recalled the blonde's comment about her and Sam getting back together, and their vehement denial. A lot of good that had done.

By morning, everyone in town would be talking, despite the fact that there was nothing to talk about. Sam would no doubt hear about it. Would he think she'd discussed the two of them with friends? He might get the wrong idea and think she cared about him. How humiliating. Amy's head started to pound for real. Suddenly she wanted out of there. She made a show of glancing at the clock under the rearview mirror. "You know, I'm late for a meeting. I'll pick up that pain reliever later." She turned on the ignition and the car purred to life. "'Bye."

SEVERAL HOURS AFTER Sam picked up Mariah and returned with her to his sister's house, his buddies Gabe and Josh knocked on the kitchen door. "We come bearing dinner," Josh announced, holding up two extra-large pizza boxes to prove it. Without waiting for an invitation, he strode into the spacious, homey kitchen. Gabe followed with a six-pack, which they'd open after Mariah went to bed.

After Sam's day, he was more than ready for a night of male companionship. He looked forward to kicking back and relaxing. "About time," he dead-panned. "Mariah's been hungry for a while now. She's about to keel over."

"I'm starving!" his niece agreed. Dancing with excitement, she rubbed her stomach and smacked her lips.

"How you doing, cuteness?" Gabe tweaked her nose on the way to the refrigerator. He stowed the beers while Josh carried the pizzas to the table in the breakfast nook.

"Grab the milk out of the fridge, will you?" Sam asked Gabe as he brought out plates and glasses.

"Milk?" Armed with napkins, Mariah wrinkled her freckled nose. "I wanted pop."

Sam's sister was a dentist, and if there was one thing he knew for certain, it was her feelings about sugared beverages. He shook his head. "Your mom likes you to drink milk."

"I know, but she's not here. Could we have pop, just this once? Pretty please?" She gave him the wide-eyed look that never failed to persuade him.

Sam shook his head. "Your mom would shoot me." Mariah's face remained hopeful, so he looked to Gabe, a family-practice doctor who just happened to take care of Mariah and her parents. "Help me out here, buddy."

The physician nodded, and the gray eyes behind his tortoiseshell glasses homed in on Mariah. "Your mom knows a thing or two about teeth. She's smart to make you drink milk," he agreed, adding his most professional nod. "You have my medical diploma on it."

"I'll throw in my CPA license, too," Josh said. He was Sam's accountant, and the best. "And, hey, what's wrong with milk? I love the stuff. Mmm, boy, milk and pizza." The dimple in his cheek deepened—a trait women seemed to find irresistible—and even Mariah was charmed.

"Okay," she said as she doled out the napkins.

Gabe poured her a glass. Then, good sport that he was, he filled the other three glasses, too.

The matching maple chair legs clattered over the tile floor as they pulled out chairs. Amid jokes and noise, they sat down. Sam opened the pizza boxes, and mouthwatering smells filled the air. He licked his lips. "How many do you want, Mariah?"

"Two," she said, holding out her plate.

Sam complied, then piled his own plate. Josh and Gabe did the same. They each dug in with gusto, and for a while no one spoke.

When only three pieces of pizza remained, Josh wiped his mouth and started the conversation with a question. "Hey, Sam, what were you and Amy doing, yelling at each other in some parking lot today?"

About to finish off his fourth slice, Sam stopped inches from his mouth. "You saw that?"

"No, but Kari Jeffries did. Now everybody knows."

Sam remembered the woman. He'd met her that first time he'd dropped Mariah at Amy's studio. He groaned. "Is there no privacy in this town?"

Mariah gaped at him. "Uncle Sam!" she scolded, clearly horrified. "Why were you fighting with my teacher? You said you liked her."

Gabe and Josh exchanged curious glances. Then Gabe shot Sam a sideways look, while Josh raised a quizzical brow. "You said that?" he asked.

Both men stared at Sam, their shock almost comical. Sam frowned. "I didn't mean it like it sounds," he said. He turned to his niece. "Amy—Miss Parker—and I weren't fighting, we were…talking." He gestured with his chin at Mariah. "Could we table this conversation until later?"

Gabe nodded. "Of course," Josh said.

Sam had known both men since grade school and could practically see the wheels turning in their cagey brains. They'd been there when he first started dating Amy, and they'd been there during and after the divorce. By the time she had moved away, they were both sick of hearing about Sam's troubles and the whole sad mess. They'd give him hell if they thought he was starting up with her again. Not that he was.

Though if they'd been privy to what had happened in her back room this afternoon… One little kiss, and he'd wanted Amy just as much as always. From her passionate response, he knew that she felt the same. Sam's body stirred at the memory. That kiss had turned into more kisses, each deeper and hotter than the last. Swallowing, he hunched over the table to hide his blatant desire. He wasn't telling anybody about those kisses, and he was pretty sure Amy wouldn't, either. Thank God for that, because neither of them would ever be able to explain or live down what they had done. How could they, when what had happened was both bewildering and impossible to understand?

"Uncle Sam?"

Mariah's voice jolted him back to the here and now. "Huh?"

She was glaring at him, so he changed the subject. "How about a bowl of chocolate ice cream and that Harry Potter video?"

Refusing to be mollified, she compressed her mouth. "Please don't fight with Miss Parker ever again."

"You have my word on that," Sam pledged solemnly. He meant it, too. He glanced at the rooster clock on the cream-colored wall. Two hours before his niece's bedtime. How would he ever survive? He stood, stacking the plates to clear the table. "If you want to watch the whole movie, we'd better get started."

BY THE TIME Sam tucked sleepy-eyed Mariah in and closed her door, he was yawning with fatigue. It had been a trying day, and he rolled his shoulders as he tromped wearily down the stairs. But he wasn't ready to send Gabe and Josh home, not until they cleared up a few things.

He grabbed three beers and carried them into the family room, where his friends sprawled in matching recliners that faced the now-dark television screen. Both accepted their drinks with grateful nods.

Sam settled on the sofa also facing the TV. He lifted his bottle in salute. "Cheers."

All three men drank. Then Gabe eyed him speculatively. "Are you going to start up with her?"

No need to ask who they meant. "Absolutely not," Sam stated. "Mariah roped me into helping out with some sets for her ballet recital. Amy and I worked on those together." No need to mention those kisses. "At the end of the day, we had a conversation." Okay, a heated conversation, but that was nobody's business. "That's all."

Josh grinned. "So you two still have that passion thing."

His dimple had no effect on Sam, who scowled.

Gabe hooted. "He's not denying it. I know you, buddy, and I can see it in your eyes. Every time you hear Amy's name, you light up."

Sam shook his head at the ceiling. "You're imagining things."

"Hell, maybe you *should* take her out," Josh said. "I mean, plenty of time has passed since the divorce, and you've both grown up a lot."

Given what Sam had put his friends through during and after his marriage, the comment surprised him. Amy was too career-oriented, too stubborn and too opinionated for him. Though in some ways she'd changed for the better, he did not want to get involved with her—now or ever. He shook his head. "Out of the question. I'm not interested, and neither is she."

"If you say so." Gabe nodded soberly but Sam

caught the glint in his eye. Josh coughed, covering up a laugh.

Sam swore. The evening was not turning out the way he'd envisioned. "She wants to get married again, and start a family. I don't."

When neither man replied, Sam narrowed his eyes. "Just because you're both happily married doesn't mean I should be. I've tried it, remember? I like being single, and I plan on staying that way. Besides, I'd make a lousy father. God knows, taking care of Mariah is just about doing me in. I don't have the patience." For emphasis, he shot each man a dark look. "Got that?"

"You're as patient as any man I know," Gabe said. "You'd make a great father, and that's my professional medical opinion."

Would he? Sam frowned and opened his mouth, but Josh spoke first.

"Hey, did either one of us mention marriage or kids?" he asked with an innocent, sideways look.

"Well, no," Sam admitted.

"We didn't bring up the subject, but you did." Gabe cocked one eyebrow, then pointed his bottle at Sam. "Think about that."

MARIAH POKED Sam's shoulder, jerking him from a deep sleep. "Uncle Sam," she whispered.

"Huh?" He opened one bleary eye. It was pitch-dark. He squinted at the clock on the bedside table.

Monday, 4:00 a.m., it read. He'd been asleep all of five hours. He fumbled for the reading lamp beside the clock, blinking in the sudden light. "What's up, kid?"

Clad in her favorite American Girl nightgown and clutching her American Girl doll in matching pj's, Mariah swallowed with difficulty. "My throat hurts."

Sam flung his arm over his eyes and groaned. "Can this wait a few hours? Say, until seven-fif-teen?"

"It hurts really bad." The girl's lower lip stuck out and her eyes filled. "I want my mom."

Sam felt like a jerk. Some uncle he was, and fur-ther proof he'd make a lousy parent. He gave an apol-ogetic smile. "Sorry kid, but you're stuck with me. Tell you what, though, we'll call her later." Scrubbing a hand over his face, he sat up. "So your throat hurts, huh?"

She nodded and sniffled. "Especially when I swallow."

Now that he thought about it, her voice sounded sort of cottony and thick, as if her throat were raw. She didn't look so good, either—pale and dull-eyed, but that could be from the early hour. Over the past few days, several of her dancer friends had come down with strep. He frowned. "You got a fever?"

"I'm pretty hot, so maybe." Her puzzled gaze wandered to his bare chest, her discomfort momentarily forgotten. "How come you're not wearing pajamas?"

Sam gave a sharp, worried glance down. Nothing visible except his chest and thighs, thank God. "I like to sleep in…my shorts," he said. His preference was to sleep naked. While taking care of Mariah, he'd opted to wear his boxers. At the moment, that seemed a very wise decision.

He smoothed down the covers and patted the bed. "Climb up." Mariah did. Sitting beside him, shoulders slumped, she stared listlessly at her lap while he felt her forehead. He frowned. "You're pretty warm. I'll call Gabe first thing in the morning and make an appointment." Sam recalled his sister's carefully written instructions for every possible emergency. He'd tacked them to the refrigerator with a large butterfly magnet. "Sit tight and I'll be right back."

He pulled on a T-shirt and headed downstairs, then grabbed the notes, skimming them on the way back to his niece. "I think you should take a couple of kids' Tylenol. Now let's get you back in your own bed."

Mariah gave a heavy nod. Hand on her narrow shoulder, he steered her down the hall to her bed.

He flipped on the light and her room lit up. His sister had decorated the space to accommodate Mariah's favorite things. Two Degas reproductions of young ballerinas hung beside a poster of a female

basketball team. Three bookshelves full of her favorite books stood over a bulging toy box. Dolls and
stuffed animals were piled high on the padded window seat that overlooked the backyard.

Sam tucked her in, then brought her the over-the-
counter pain reliever—liquid because she didn't like
pills—and a glass of ice water. Obediently she swallowed the medicine, chasing it with water.

"Will I have to miss school?" she asked, her eyes
large and worried.

"Probably." Which meant he'd miss work. Along
with his normal busy Monday, he was about to bid
on property for a new Cutter's in a small town up
the freeway. He was also in the middle of negotiat-
ing with a new meat vendor. With his calendar full
of meetings and appointments, he couldn't afford to
stay home. But what choice did he have? Luckily
he'd brought his laptop home.

"If you have to go to work, Claudia can probably baby-sit me when she gets home from school,"
Mariah said as if she'd read his mind.

"Good idea." Sam nodded. He'd contact her.

"You'll have to call my teacher and get the homework. And Miss Parker, too, and tell her I won't be
at rehearsal."

Given what had happened a few days earlier,
Sam didn't relish the idea of talking to Amy. He had
enough trouble keeping his thoughts off her without conducting an actual conversation. He'd take

care of the problem with a crack-of-dawn call, and leave a message on her machine. Then again, knowing her workaholic tendencies, she'd likely be at work first thing. He couldn't stop a groan.

"Uncle Sam?" Mariah eyed him, still worried, but with a sleepy look.

"I'll talk to her," he grumbled. "Now try to go back to sleep."

Sam didn't bother. He was showered and dressed by five-thirty. Too early to phone anyone. He turned on the coffeemaker, setting up the laptop while the coffee brewed. The fragrant smell helped him wake up. He logged on to his office computer, savoring his first cup while he took care of e-mails. Then he refilled his mug, ate a bowl of cereal and scanned the newspaper. He made his first call at seven, to Gabe.

"Bring her in at nine," his friend said.

Next, Sam phoned work. His secretary, a punctual and efficient woman in her mid-fifties, arrived daily at seven-fifteen. They worked through his calendar, rescheduling the day's activities. "I'll get back to you later this morning," he pledged forty-five minutes later.

It was nearly time to wake Mariah. After her rough night, he hated to do that. He'd let her sleep a while longer and use the time to call Amy. With dread, Sam looked up the number, which his sister had provided along with dozens of other numbers relating to Mariah and her activities. Not that he actually needed to consult the list. Though he hadn't phoned Amy in over a decade and hadn't planned to, he'd memorized both her studio and home numbers. Knowing that didn't brighten his mood any. Stern-lipped, he grabbed the phone and with an odd mixture of dread and anticipation he didn't understand, punched in the number to the studio.

After six rings, the machine clicked on, which caught Sam by surprise. Years back, Amy had started work first thing every morning. She would have been at the studio by now.

Ignoring a stab of disappointment he released a relieved breath. At least he didn't have to talk to her. He left a message, then went to wake his niece.

"Sorry Claudia can't come over today," Mariah said after dutifully taking her first dose of the prescription medication Gabe had ordered. She lay listlessly on the sofa, watching a kids' TV show.

"Hey, you can't help it," Sam said.

Gabe had cultured her throat, but one look at the redness and blisters and he knew. She had strep. According to Gabe, she was contagious for the first twenty-four hours after starting her medication. She'd miss at least one more day of school.

His niece yawned. "I think I'll take a nap."

Sam clicked off the TV and nodded. "I'll be in the kitchen, working. Holler if you need me."

He checked his voice mail. Amy had phoned, reminding him that it was his turn to bring the refreshments on Saturday. Sounding suitably sympathetic, she'd also she wished Mariah a speedy recovery. Nice of her, Sam thought. Though nice didn't begin to describe Amy. Elbow on the table, he woke up his computer and stared at the screen without seeing it. How would he describe her? he mused. Full of fire, beautiful, passionate, one hell of a kisser—midthought he frowned and stopped himself. Their relationship, if you could call it that, was headed nowhere. And he'd wasted way too much time thinking about her. Besides, he had work to do.

Mariah slept on and off. Between fixing lunch, getting her assignments from her teacher and keeping her company when she was awake, Sam managed to conduct a fair amount of business via phone and e-mail. By late afternoon, his niece felt well enough to work on her homework. Then they played Monopoly. Sam let her win. With the kid in better spirits, taking care of her wasn't so bad.

Just before he tucked her in for the night, she smiled. "You're just as fun as my dad."

The words surprised him. Sam angled her a look. "I'll take that as a compliment."

She nodded. "You could be a daddy, too, Uncle Sam. Then I'd have a cousin. She'd think you were the best dad ever."

High praise, coming from his niece. "Thanks,

kid." Sam had never imagined himself in that role. He didn't believe he had the temperament, despite Gabe's pronouncement the other night that he did. "Being your uncle is good enough for me."

But later, just before falling asleep, he mulled over Mariah's words and their day. For a guy with scant experience taking care of kids, especially a sick kid, he'd done okay. It might be fun to have one of his own. Too bad he'd never get married.

The unexpected thought garnered a scowl. The single life was what he wanted. He'd get his "kid" fix through his niece.

THANKS TO THE WONDERS of modern medicine, by dinner on Tuesday Mariah seemed good as new, and ready to head back to school and resume her activities. Sam marveled at her quick recovery, which included a hearty appetite and the return of her natural exuberance. He watched with amusement as she demolished the chocolate sundae he'd made for dessert at her request.

"Friday is show-and-tell," she said when she at last came up for air. "I want to bring you."

"What for?"

Turning her head sideways, she wrinkled her nose as if the question were ridiculous. "As my show-and-tell, silly."

Having missed two days at the office, Sam didn't relish missing yet more work. "Is that allowed?"

Mariah licked the chocolate from her spoon before replying. "I'll ask my teacher. Some of the other kids in my class have brought in special people, so I know she'll say yes. The kids will think it's so cool to meet the owner of Cutter's Fabulous Burgers."

"Special, huh?"

She positively glowed with pride as she nodded, which pleased Sam. That plus her hopeful, big-eyed look made her request difficult to refuse.

He shrugged. "I think I can make that. Maybe I'll hand out coupons for Cutter's specials, too. Ask your teacher about that."

"I will!" Mariah's toothy grin told him he'd said the right thing.

"WHAT'S IT LIKE, eating Cutter's burgers, fries and shakes any time you want?" a pudgy boy with curly brown hair asked Sam during show-and-tell.

The question was exactly what a growing boy would want to know. Sam's mouth quirked. During his half hour here, he had fielded half a dozen similar questions from Mariah's two dozen classmates. "I don't eat every meal at my restaurant," he said. "But I do eat lunch at one Cutter's or another almost every day."

"You're so lucky," a pink-cheeked girl wearing a braided headband said with an envious sigh.

Everyone in class seemed to agree, evidenced by the sudden escalation in noise level.

Sam grinned. This was easy, and fun, too.

"There's time for two more questions and then we'll let Mr. Cutter get back to running his business," said Mariah's teacher, a string bean of a middle-aged woman.

"Can I have your autograph?" a kid with big ears and a large mouth asked.

"May I," the teacher corrected.

The boy flushed. "May I have your autograph, Mr. Cutter?" he repeated.

"Sure," Sam replied. "I have some restaurant coupons, too, which I'll give your teacher to hand out."

A tow-headed girl from Mariah's dance group, whose name Sam didn't recall, raised her hand. He nodded to her to speak.

"Is it true you and Miss Parker used to be married?"

Sam hadn't anticipated the question. Not here, and not from a pip-squeak of a girl. He rolled his eyes. Was there no escape from the gossip? "A long time ago."

"Before I was born," Mariah added sagely as she cut Sam a curious look.

"Are you going to marry her again?" the pudgy boy asked.

This kid wasn't even a dancer. Sam shook his head. "Absolutely not." Frowning, he looked to the teacher for help.

The pesky female dancer opened her mouth. "But, my mom said—"

"Looks like we're out of time," Sam cut in. He moved aside as the red-faced teacher walked to the front of the room.

She cleared her throat and shot Sam an I'm-sorry-they-got-personal smile. "Let's thank Mariah for bringing her uncle, and thank Mr. Cutter for his time and the coupons."

The class dutifully voiced their appreciation. Sam nodded and beat a hasty retreat.

Some show-and-tell.

Chapter Six

THE FOLLOWING SATURDAY, Amy stood at the side of the stage directing the Rubies—sixteen eleven- and twelve-year-olds, tall, short, chubby and thin—as they worked through the end of their dance. Due to a nasty strep bug that had circulated through the group, more than a few students had missed several days of rehearsal. In their short time away, they'd already forgotten parts of their routine. "Adagio, and pirouette," she reminded them to the rousing beat of a Mozart piano concerto. "One and two, and move into high fifth."

Faces taut with concentration, they executed the final steps in time to the music, some in sync, others a beat behind. The dance ended with a dramatic crescendo. In the moment of silence following, flushed and breathless, the entire group glanced expectantly toward Amy.

They'd worked hard, and while they were far

from good, Amy was satisfied. "Nice job," she proclaimed with a pleased smile.

Grins broke out everywhere. "Yes!" exclaimed Jared Shorey, a reedy, thin twelve-year-old. Fists of agreement shot into the air, and excited chatter erupted as the dancers on stage and those sitting on the floor out front shared their exuberance. Forty-four students in all, they created a lot of noise.

Amy let them talk. Everyone had been respectful and quiet throughout the Rubies' rehearsal. Now they needed a chance to let loose. With only three weeks until the recital, she'd started a four-hour rehearsal this morning. Each group had run through their routines several times while kids from the other groups watched. Since Amy wanted the recital to be a surprise for the parents, adults were no longer allowed to stay and watch. The kids loved sharing a secret, and the mystery created a wonderful buzz of excitement.

Amy was excited, too, but she needed a break. She glanced at the large round clock opposite the mirrored wall. Nearly lunchtime, thank goodness. "May I have your attention, dancers?" She called out, holding up a hand. When silence fell and the attention focused on her she continued. "That's it until after lunch. We'll take an hour's break, and then we'll run through our group finale. After that, some of your parents will be here to work on the things we need for the recital. But you get to go home."

"Hey, Mariah, when is your uncle bringing the food?" David Smith asked, peering at the girl from the stage. At twelve, he was growing like a weed and always hungry.

This was Sam's and Mariah's day to provide the snack. Sam had generously offered to feed the whole group at his expense, a proposal too good to refuse. From her place on the floor Mariah shifted positions and studied the clock, her expression worried. "He *said* he'd be here at noon." Frowning, she looked to Amy. "Should we call him, Miss Parker?"

The man had his faults, but he always followed through. "I'm sure he'll be here," Amy assured the girl. "This is a good time to wash up and find a place to sit."

Noisy conversation resumed. Laughing, talking, and exuberant, the Rubies skipped, loped and moved en masse across the stage with a boundless energy that Amy envied.

Her shoulders slumped as she fast-forwarded the tape of recital music she'd recorded to the finale piece she'd need later. She was worn down, and not just because of the rehearsal schedule. She'd also fielded endless questions about the performance from both parents and kids. Then there were the whispers, blatant stares and speculative comments about her and Sam. Just as Amy had feared, Kari and Connie had spread untrue rumors all over town. Over and over, she'd explained that there was nothing between her and Sam. They were not getting back together, didn't plan to in the future and never would. People seemed to listen. They nodded, but Amy got the feeling they didn't believe her. Even Dani and Nina seemed skeptical. Her best friends!

It didn't matter that she and Sam had given them nothing to work from. They'd barely spoken since last Saturday. Sure, he'd come in twice to work on the sets. But there were other parents around, and they plainly observed that nothing at all passed between her and Sam other than a brief hello. Why couldn't people stop manufacturing ridiculous things that weren't true? Amy was truly perturbed. With all the rumors floating around, she'd never meet a man to make a life with. The rumors had to stop.

No doubt Sam had heard the same kinds of comments. Amy planned to talk to him when he delivered lunch. They needed to compare notes and figure out how to put an end to the gossip. With parents not allowed in the studio for another two hours and the students wrapped up in the recital and their own lives, a private discussion with Sam should be safe enough.

"He's here!" Mariah shouted over the noise. "Hi, Uncle Sam!" She jumped up and dashed toward the door at the back of the room.

All heads turned toward Sam. Arms heavy with two flats of pop, he shouldered open the door. Sunlight slipped through as two high school boys trudged inside hefting large boxes. Sam followed, letting the door bang shut behind him.

He looked straight at Amy, who waited near the stage. "Where do you want this stuff?" he asked over the noise.

"Up here by the stage."

Trailed by the two gawky boys, Sam strode forward, his biceps bulging from his load. Amy told herself not to look at his strong arms wearing that gray T-shirt, but how could she help herself? Her heart thudded giddily in her chest and her stomach did a funny flip-flop—the same unwanted visceral response she had every time she saw him.

Several girls from the Rubies and Emeralds shyly eyed Sam's young assistants. Though the nine-through twelve-year-old females were far too young for teenage boys, both males noticed and flushed scarlet. They set their boxes on the stage, then shoved their hands in their pockets and shifted awkwardly. Sam thanked them, then tipped both generously and sent them on their way.

The aromas of French fries, onion rings and piping hot burgers quickly filled the air. The noise level increased as hungry kids crowded around. Sam caught Amy's eye and shook his head at the growing pandemonium. *Kids*, he seemed to be saying. *I know,* Amy shrugged, and for one brief moment they were on the same wavelength.

She smiled, and then so did he, even his eyes. His whole face lit up, and suddenly he was more than a good-looking man. He was irresistible. Amy succumbed completely to his charm. For the second time since he'd walked through the door, her heart expanded. Touching her hand to her chest, she drew in a dreamy breath. As she released a sigh, his grin subtly shifted to an intimate smile meant just for her. His eyes darkened and warmed. Pure, unadulterated heat seemed to arc between them. Blood rushed to Amy's face, and she quickly ducked her head. She sensed that Sam, too, had averted his gaze.

She simply must put a stop to this ridiculous physical upheaval whenever he was nearby. He wasn't the man for her, and she wasn't right for him. Hadn't history proved that?

The kids were swarming around the food like bees, and she hurried forward. "Dancers, listen up. We need to thank Mr. Cutter for providing lunch."

"Thank you," the group replied in unison.

Sam dipped his chin in a mock bow. "My pleasure."

Satisfied, Amy continued. "I want you all to line up," she directed in a loud voice. "Pearls first, then Emeralds, and then Rubies. Mr. Cutter will hand out the burgers and either onion rings or fries. After you have your food, choose a drink. Then please find a seat on the floor."

"Why do the Pearls go first?" someone grumbled.

"Because they're the youngest," Amy replied. She pointed to the floor near Sam. "The line starts here."

Boys and girls moved into place. Amy stayed at the end of the line, keeping an eye on things. She watched Sam hand out the food. To her surprise, he looked as if he enjoyed the job, offering jokes and comments to each child. He seemed genuinely to like the kids, and they knew it. As the line inched forward, several dancers hung around him, watching his every move. The girls simpered and giggled, and the boys emulated his stance, legs splayed, back straight. Clearly they adored him.

At the moment, who wouldn't? He was great with kids, a trait she'd never imagined he possessed. He'd make a great daddy. It seemed a shame he didn't want to settle down and start a family, be-cause—appalled at the direction of her thoughts, Amy stopped her musing point-blank. Sam had set aside a veggie burger, and she thanked him. She wanted to walk away, but needed to discuss the gossip and how to stop it. "Could I talk to you a minute?" she asked.

He looked surprised and not exactly pleased. "What about?"

His reaction stung until she remembered that she wasn't thrilled about talking to him, either. But this was important. She glanced around, making sure the students weren't listening. Keeping her voice low, she explained. "People are talking." She flushed. "About us."

"There is no 'us'," Sam said, but his pained expression told her he knew exactly what she meant. "Why can't they get that?"

Amy shook her head. "I don't know, but if they keep talking, neither of us will ever get a date again. We need a game plan, something that will stop the gossip."

"Sounds like a good idea." Sam nodded. He glanced around the room, filled with kids. "Where can we talk?"

Amy considered her office, but she wanted to be within supervising distance of the group.

"Over there." She gestured toward the empty bench along the mirrored wall. "Come on."

Sam grabbed an extra burger and joined her.

SAM SWUNG ONE LEG over the hard, narrow bench and faced Amy. Not ten feet away a horde of kids ate, chattered, and laughed, making enough noise to fill the room. They weren't talking about him and Amy, the way their parents were—for now. He was still in shock over the questions and comments from the kids in Mariah's class, who all seemed to know about him and Amy. Not that there was anything to know. He wanted to talk to her about that, but after his morning he was starving. He'd dropped Mariah at rehearsal, mowed the lawn and then, feeling restless, he'd run three miles. All before eleven.

He bit into a bacon cheeseburger, savoring the flavor of high-quality, charbroiled beef. Ten years in the fast-food business and he still relished the food. Amy, who, unlike him, did not straddle the bench, seemed hungry, too. She dug into her veggie burger with obvious enjoyment. Despite the mess they seemed to be in, they both enjoyed the meal—created by the burger chain he had founded. Pride swelled in his chest.

"I am so sick of everyone talking and whispering about us," she said after a while.

Sam nodded as he swallowed a mouthful. "Sometimes living in a small town is a real pain," he said over the noise. "Even Josh and Gabe are giving me a hard time."

"You, too? Dani and Nina keep dropping hints about how we've both changed and that maybe we should think about getting together again." She shook her head. "Can you believe that?"

Sam's mouth tightened. "Why should *we* have to do anything? We're not the ones jumping to false conclusions."

"You're saying we should ignore the talk? Given that it's going on all day, everywhere I go, that's not so easy."

Suddenly the noise level fell. Sam glanced at the young dancers sprawled across the floor. Several curious faces were turned their way. He swore under his breath. "Even the kids are talking," he said, keeping his voice below their range of hearing. Noting Mariah's speculative look, he glanced upward and shook his head. "My own niece is the worst." Since the disastrous show-and-tell day at her school, she'd been pestering him about dating Amy, and no amount of stern conversation stemmed her enthusiasm. His appetite ruined, Sam frowned and pushed aside his lunch. "I'll be glad when her parents get back."

"I'm sure you will." Amy sighed and carefully folded the wrapping around her half-eaten sandwich. "This is a definite problem, and unless we do something it's not going away." She set the food on the bench beside his. "We need a plan of action."

"So we do." Sam rubbed his chin and considered various options. "Maybe we should give them something to talk about." Where had *that* brilliant idea come from?

"What?" Amy said in a loud voice. Now every kid in the place stared openly.

"It was a joke," he fabricated.

"Well, it wasn't funny."

"So sue me." He shot a glance at the wide-eyed kids and scowled. "I can't discuss this in front of them. We'll finish this conversation after they're gone."

"How? You'll have Mariah with you."

"She's going home with Delia Jeffries so I can work more on the sets. They've invited her to stay overnight."

Amy groaned. "Oh, no. Delia's mother started all this—with Connie's input."

"I know, I know." Sam gave a helpless shrug. "But Mariah really wanted to go home with Delia. I didn't even try to talk her out of it. She'd just argue until she got her way." The noise level increased and he saw that most of the kids, his niece included, seemed to have lost interest in him and Amy in favor of eating and talking among themselves. "Besides, I could use a night off." Much as he loved his niece, caring for her was exhausting. He needed a break and looked forward to a meal without her.

Amy gave an understanding nod. "At least Connie will be here later to help with the sets. She can't spread rumors about us while she's working alongside us."

"I suppose that compensates for spending time with her," Sam commented drily. He glanced at the wall clock. "I should be going. What time should I come back?"

"Everyone else will be here at three-thirty, after we rehearse the group finale."

Sam nodded. He swung his leg over the bench and stood. "I'll be back at three then, and we'll talk."

SITTING AT THE DESK in her closet-sized office, Amy cupped the phone to her ear and frowned. "I'm sorry your dog is sick," she told Kelly Margolis, one of the parent volunteers who was supposed to be here in half an hour. Rehearsals had ended a short while ago, and all the dancers were gone. "I'll see you Tuesday afternoon, instead." Frowning, she hung up.

Amy's hip ached and she massaged it absently as she pondered the situation. That made six of the eight expected volunteers who had called to reschedule this afternoon's work party. Over the past half hour, she had heard a dazzling array of excuses from, "Something unexpected came up," to "I think I'm coming down with the flu," to "I accidentally double-booked myself and can't get out of the other commitment." The only two who hadn't cancelled were Connie and Sam. Obviously something was in the works. But what? Baffled, Amy shoved a hand under her braid and rubbed her nape.

From her seat, she heard the door to the studio open. Three o'clock on the nose. Solid footsteps moved steadily across the wooden floor. Even if she hadn't expected Sam, she knew that self-assured gait. She let out a relieved breath. She'd never imagined *wanting* to see him, but with all the cancellations, she both needed and welcomed his help. "In here," she called.

He appeared in the threshold. Bracing his shoulder against the doorjamb, he cocked his hip. "Ready to finish that talk?"

Amy nodded. She couldn't help noting how Sam's pose caused his T-shirt to pull tightly over his chest and flat belly. Did the man have any idea how sexy he looked? Against her will, she glanced lower, to the healthy bulge of his manhood. Well-endowed, and he wasn't even aroused. Of course then, he *really* was something…

"Amy?"

She jerked her attention to his knowing eyes and quirking mouth. Her cheeks burned. Unnerved by the train of her thoughts and by the fact that he seemed to be reading her mind, she scowled. "What?"

He sobered immediately. "Are you too busy to talk, after all?" he asked, misinterpreting her unhappy expression.

That was just fine with her. "No, just puzzled. There's something odd going on. Nearly every volunteer has backed out until next week." Propping her head on her hand, she sighed. "I'm afraid it's just you, me and Connie this afternoon."

"She can't make it, either." Sam pushed away from the jamb. "She paged me a few minutes ago. Something about her ex not being able to take their daughter this afternoon. Said to tell you she'll be here Monday and Tuesday afternoon, instead."

"Lovely," Amy muttered as the last of her plans for a large work party evaporated. "That's the trouble with volunteers. They don't always follow through."

"Hey, things happen." He shrugged. "Sometimes you have to roll with the changes."

He sounded so…easygoing. Not at all like the in-control Sam Amy remembered. Unbelieving, she gaped at him.

"What?" he asked, frowning.

"Twelve years ago, a sudden change in plans would have really thrown you. You've changed."

One shoulder shrugged. "Chalk that up to owning a business and learning a thing or two about life. Just call me Mr. Older and Wiser."

"I know what you mean," Amy said. Mindful of her aching hip, she rose slowly, wincing despite her care.

A knowing look of concern filled his face. "Still getting those charley horses?"

During their marriage she'd had quite a few muscle spasms, mostly in her calves or feet. Many dancers suffered from the same ailment. But she was the only one lucky enough to be treated by "Dr. Sam." First, he'd massage away the cramp, then tenderly kiss the sore spot. He'd keep right on touching and kissing, his lips and hands inflaming her to a frenzy of need. The red-hot sex that always followed magically erased her aches and pains.

Sam's eyes warmed and darkened, and Amy knew he remembered as well. She swallowed and looked down at her desk, and the moment passed.

"I'm afraid this isn't a charley horse," she said as she kneaded the muscle. "It's an old dance injury, and the reason I gave up dancing professionally."

Sam rubbed his chin appraisingly. "I wondered why you quit."

"That's only part of the reason." She gave a wry smile. "I turn thirty next spring, and in the dance business, that's old."

"You don't look old to me." His gaze roved boldly over her, and she couldn't help straightening her back, sucking in her stomach and raising her head. "You look great."

A flush of pleasure warmed her face. "Um, thanks."

"You're welcome."

For an uncomfortable moment that felt like forever, they studied each other. In the past, they'd either fought or made love, rarely just talked. This felt new and awkward. But also very good. Amy tried a smile. "Do you realize this is the first time in a very long time that we've actually talked without ending up in an argument?"

Sam offered his own smile. "Proof of our maturity." He glanced over his shoulder, toward the stage. "We may as well get some work done." He gestured Amy through the door, and together they headed for the storage room. "Guess it's just you and me again."

The words reminded her about the gossip. She groaned. "I can just imagine what everyone will say about that."

"We'll get so much done, they won't dare talk," Sam said. "Besides, we're not interested in each other and we're not dating. We should be able to work on the sets together. As friends. We can discuss how to handle the gossip while we work."

He'd brought up a point Amy had never considered. "Do you think we *could* be friends?"

"I'm willing to try." Sam angled his chin her way and raised one brow as if to ask: Are you?

That was enough for Amy. She nodded. "Then, so am I."

"That's my girl."

They grinned at each other—warm, open, friendly smiles. As they walked toward the stage, Sam slung his arm around her shoulders and tugged her to his side. Familiar warmth filled her and, as naturally as breathing, she leaned into him.

For the first time in a long while, she felt content. With Sam, the man who had broken her heart. That scared her, and her step faltered.

"Careful of that hip," he warned, mistaking her hesitation for discomfort. "Let me take your weight." He lowered his arm to her waist and guided her forward.

Suddenly the painful past loomed in front of her. Did Sam want something from her? Was he trying to take charge of her? She shot him a wary glance. His unguarded expression was relaxed and pleasant. Not sexual, stubborn or angry. A friend helping a friend.

Reassured, Amy relaxed.

KARI PICKED UP the wall phone on the first ring, turning her back on the rest of the kitchen. "Is that you, Connie?" she whispered, feeling deliciously sneaky.

"Yes," Connie replied in a tinny sound that meant she was using her car speakerphone and that there were no kids around. "Why are you whispering?"

"Just playing it safe." Kari glanced over her shoulder, confirming there was no one else in her spacious kitchen. "Delia and Mariah are in the other room," she continued in a low voice, "but I don't want to take a chance on their listening in." In the distance, she heard the sound of laughter. Clearly the girls were not listening. Still, for good measure, she carried the phone into the pantry and closed the door. "Well?"

"I just cruised by the studio," Connie replied. "It's been two hours now, and Sam's car is still parked beside Amy's. And there are no other vehicles on the premises," she added, sounding as professional as a detective.

Kari grinned. "Our little conspiracy seems to be working." They'd held an impromptu meeting with several parents. All agreed that Sam and Amy needed to spend the afternoon alone.

Her friend chuckled. "Aren't we clever?"

"Actually…" Kari bit her lip. "I feel a little guilty. Amy would surely kill us if she suspected what we've done. And Sam…" She let the words trail off. Who knew how that gorgeous, sexy man might react to their meddling? She heard Connie's sharp intake of breath and pictured her stern look.

"Listen here, Kari, Sam and Amy belong together. You know it, and I know it. Heck, even our kids know it. The way they look at each other and the sizzle between them. If you could have *seen* them working on the sets last weekend…I'm not used to being ignored, especially when I flirt. But for all the attention Sam paid me, I may as well not have been there. He only has eyes for Amy." Connie sighed. "Just thinking about that makes me go woozy inside."

She had a point. When Sam and Amy were in the same room, the air around them seemed charged with an invisible current. It was so darn romantic. "I know what you mean," Kari replied, leaning dreamily against a shelf of canned goods.

"But they're both hardheaded. The way things are going, neither of them is ever going to act on those feelings," Connie continued. "*Someone* had to give them a push. We're doing the right thing here, and some day they'll thank us." She paused. "If they ever find out what we did."

"I certainly won't tell." Though her friend couldn't see her, Kari pretended to turn a key over her lips.

"Me, neither. I wonder what they're doing right now."

Kari frowned at the suggestive timbre of Connie's voice. "That's none of our business."

"It is if we want them back together. Did you get in touch with Amy's friends?"

"Nina and Dani? Yes. They had plans to meet at Amy's for dinner tonight. They should be phoning her any minute now to cancel."

"Do you think Amy and Sam will have dinner?"

"Let's hope." Kari crossed her fingers. "Nina says when she cancels, she'll plant the idea without directly coming out and saying it."

"Okay," Connie said. "We'll just have to hope that works."

Chapter Seven

PERCHED ON AN old wooden stool, Amy leaned over the worktable and carefully squirted hot glue over the plywood "roof" of the two-dimensional cottage Sam had made. Behind her and across the room, he wielded a paintbrush on a group of tall particle-board mushrooms and flowers.

They'd been working for a while now. Since their agreement to be platonic friends, the tension between them had shifted into an easy, relaxed mode. Now and then, one of them started a conversation, but so far, neither felt compelled to talk. During the stretches of silence, which weren't at all uncomfortable, soft jazz from the radio filled in the quiet. From time to time, Sam whistled in accompaniment. Amy couldn't remember ever hearing him whistle. She couldn't recall ever feeling this comfortable around him, either.

This friendship thing was a good idea.

"I told you that my parents are retired and living

in Florida," she said as she quickly affixed a handful of straw "thatch" to the glue. "What about yours? Do they still live on the edge of town?"

Sam jerked his attention from his work. "Not since the divorce. Mom bought a condo in California, where she has family. Pop lives in a cabin at the foothills of the Cascade Mountains, about seventy-five miles from here."

Amy's eyes widened at the surprising news. "I hadn't heard about their divorce. I'm sorry."

"When it happened seven years ago, I was, too," he said, with a regretful expression. "You know how it was. Mom ran the house, but Pop ran her. Turns out, he was too demanding. She couldn't take it anymore." He paused, his paintbrush swish-swishing over the particleboard.

"I never realized any of that," Amy said. "I thought they were happy."

But suddenly things fell into place. Sam had admired his father and had idealized his parents' marriage. He'd always talked about it. It made sense that he'd model his behavior as a husband on his father's actions—behavior that had rankled Amy no end.

The insight stunned her. How had she missed something so huge? She thought about commenting on her sudden revelation, but refrained. She and Sam were getting along so well, and she didn't want to jinx that.

"It's funny," Sam said without a trace of humor.

She checked to make sure the glue had set, then pivoted in her chair to face him. "What?"

"I always thought they had the perfect arrangement." He set aside one brush and picked up another, dipping it into a can of black paint.

When she remained silent, his attention returned to his painting. "I know exactly what you're thinking," he said. "That I wanted our marriage to work the same as my folks." He paused and met her eye. "That was a mistake."

The frank admission—that he was wrong—stunned her. Another new facet to the man. "Wow." She arched and lowered her eyebrows. "Who are you, and what have you done with Sam?"

Her question garnered a shrug and a self-deprecating smirk. "You're not the same, either. What happened to that career-driven woman?"

"Oh, I still love dance. I always will. But my priorities have shifted. I want a family now, a husband, kids and the white picket fence."

"So you said a while back." His mouth set as he painted black spots on a red mushroom cap. "I think you could do both very well," he said. His gaze raised to hers. "*If* you can find the right man."

His eyes issued a challenge that maybe she couldn't, but Amy chose to ignore that and focus on the positive. "Oh, I'll find him," she stated.

His expression neutral, Sam nodded thoughtfully.

Amy noted the slight tensing of his jaw and the sudden compression of his mouth. That puzzled her. Was he upset that she wanted to settle down? No, she decided. Why should he be? She was letting their rocky past interfere with their new relationship. She continued. "I appreciate your vote of confidence that I can successfully combine a family and my career."

Sam shrugged a thank-you. Not an ounce of tension, either. Amy released a breath of relief. She'd definitely imagined that he was upset. She smiled at him. "What about you, Sam? How come you never got married again?"

He shot her an incredulous frown. "Do I look like an idiot?" he asked, his voice dripping sarcasm.

Obviously she'd said the wrong thing. Amy sniffed. "You don't have to get hostile about it."

"Well, it was a ridiculous question. Being married to you was no picnic, honey. One ride through hell is enough for me." He snorted. "More than enough."

Things between them had been bad, even miserable at times. But hell? She'd made his life hell? As if he hadn't contributed a big chunk of misery himself. Insulted and stung, she bristled. Then she glared at him. He glared back and just like that, the tension returned, crackling uncomfortably between them.

"You make it sound as if I'm responsible for our

bad marriage," she accused. Sam's eyes narrowed a fraction, the way they did when he was spoiling for an argument.

She knew she should stop right there, but couldn't seem to restrain herself. Crossing her arms over her chest, she eyed him. "Well, it wasn't exactly paradise for me, either. What you just said about me making your life hell was plain-out spiteful. Is it that you're insensitive, or do you have some other agenda?" Her voice shook and she realized she was quaking with emotion.

"Agenda?" He scrubbed a hand over his face, smearing black paint on his chin. A look of astonishment filled his face, as if he truly hadn't realized that his words had stung. "I'm not insensitive. You're just too damn sensitive. Always were."

"No, I'm not," she said, but her lips started to tremble, and thick tears gathered behind her eyes. After Sam's comment, there was no way she would cry in front of him. There was nothing to cry over, anyway. He was right, she *was* too sensitive. She blinked furiously.

"Here we go again," he muttered, tossing aside the paintbrush. "So much for trying to be friends."

Amy dropped her shaking hands to her lap and locked them together. "That's one point we definitely agree on."

Suddenly the cell phone she had placed on the worktable rang. This was her personal line, the one

only family and friends used. Thankful for the inter-
ruption, she snatched it up. "Hello?" she said as she
pivoted on the stool, turning her back to Sam.

"It's me," said Nina.

"And me," Dani chimed in. "We're using the
three-way line. Are you still at the studio?"

"Unfortunately, yes. But I've had more than
enough. I'm leaving shortly," she announced for
Sam's benefit.

Behind her she heard paintbrushes plop into a can
of water.

"How many parents showed up?"

"Not a single one."

"You're alone?" Nina asked, her tone curious. "I
didn't expect—"

"Sam's here," Amy interrupted, not bothering to
hide her unhappiness. "Listening to my every
word."

She heard his snort of annoyance, could feel his
eyes on her. Let him stare. She stiffened her spine
and lifted her head so that her braid brushed across
her back reassuringly.

"Ah," Dani said. "Isn't that interesting?"

"No, it is not," Amy snapped.

"So you're not getting along?" Nina asked with
what sounded like regret.

Why did she sound like that? The days for despair over what could have been between her and
Sam were long gone. "Definitely not." She frowned

at a bare spot on the cottage roof. It needed more straw. Cupping the receiver between her ear and shoulder she grabbed the glue gun. "What's up?"

"Bad news," Dani said. "Neither Nina nor I can make it tonight."

"Oh." Amy couldn't stifle her disappointment. She squirted two lines of glue over the empty spots on the roof, then added the straw, pressing until the glue set. "Why not?"

"My future in-laws invited us over tonight," Nina sighed. "I can't believe I forgot that. This wedding has wiped out my memory."

"Russ's brother and wife just called," Dani said. "Remember how I told you they were driving over from Seattle tomorrow morning? Well, they surprised us by pulling into town a few minutes ago—with ribs and homemade barbecue sauce for dinner. I am so sorry."

"We both are," Nina said.

Amy was, too, but this was nobody's fault. She forced nonchalance. "Things happen," she said quoting Sam.

She sensed his reaction—curiosity and surprise.

"I hate for you to spend the evening alone," Nina added. "With the moon in Cancer, that's not a good idea. You need company, especially during dinner. Is there someone you could eat with?"

Sam came to mind. Half an hour ago, Amy would have considered inviting him over, two friends sharing dinner. She wasn't about to do that now. She sighed. "No," she said, shaking her head. "No one."

HEADED ACROSS THE STAGE Sam had to move fast to keep pace with Amy. Tight-lipped, head high and attention straight ahead, she was clearly mad as she clipped toward the exit. Well, he couldn't say he hadn't suffered through her anger before. Suffer being the key word.

Back when they were married, their arguments had turned his world dark and miserable. Sam could never breathe normally until he'd smoothed things over, usually with great sex. He glanced sideways at Amy, who stiffened as if she sensed his gaze. No chance of fixing things with sex now. Not that he wanted to make love with Amy. At that lie, his lip curled in self-derision. Sure, he desired her, but he didn't intend to act on his need.

He wanted the friendship, though, and had actually imagined they could be friends. He'd enjoyed working alongside her this afternoon. She'd seemed to share the sentiment. Until he'd screwed up things.

Without a word, Amy suddenly veered into her small office, where she retrieved her purse. Sam waited, shifting uncomfortably. With his sarcastic comment equating their marriage with hell and blaming her, he'd wrecked the fragile, easygoing relationship they'd started to forge. But when she'd talked about settling down with some guy and starting a family… He'd hated that. His strong feelings bothered him. Frowning, he ground the toe of his sneaker against the wood floor. So what if she wanted to get married again? That was no concern of his. He felt like a total jerk deliberately upsetting her.

Amy swished past him, leaving behind a faint scent of vanilla. Without a backward glance, she marched to the exit. Sam swore under his breath. He would apologize and try to smooth the way toward friendship. He lengthened his stride, and they reached the exit at the same time. Amy grabbed the doorknob.

"Wait." Sam laid his hand over hers. Quickly she jerked away, but not before he'd felt the fine tremors that shook her. He knew what that meant: she still was upset. "Please," he added.

She huffed an irritated breath. To his relief she finally looked at him, though warily. "What?"

Apologies didn't come easily, and he rubbed his neck as he searched for a way to make things right. "I meant what I said about being friends," he said at last.

Amy's brows arched in wry surprise, but her eyes were cool and unforgiving. "Could have fooled me."

She wasn't making this easy. Sam groaned. "Give me a break, Amy. I'm trying to apologize." He tensed as she absorbed his statement and considered it, relaxed when she nodded.

"Just why is being friends so important to you?" she asked, tilting her face toward him.

With her eyes large and searching, and her lower lip pinned by her teeth, she was incredibly attractive. The strong urge to nibble that lower lip himself, then kiss her senseless grabbed hold of Sam. Yeah, right. That hadn't exactly solved their problems in the past, and it was the wrong solution to this mess. He curled his hands at his sides. "To prove we can do it. Not just to ourselves, but to everybody in town. Also because we should have been friends before, and we never were." They'd been too busy with fighting and making up to cultivate a real relationship. "Besides, I enjoyed this afternoon. Admit it, you did, too."

"Most of it," she conceded.

"Then we're back on track?"

"If it's that important to you, why not?" She threw up her hands, but the soft light in her eyes belied her tone. She wanted this friendship as much as he did.

Sam grinned. He didn't understand his euphoric relief any more than the words that slipped from his mouth. "Have dinner with me tonight. I'll cook."

Her mouth twitched in amusement. "Define *cook*."

At least she hadn't turned him down. "I'm talking about a genuine, home-cooked meal. From scratch." It wouldn't be fancy, but he could make salad, bake two potatoes and grill a couple of steaks. "I've been staying at my sister's, so that's where we'll eat." He could have taken her to his place, but that was his private refuge. Except for family, he didn't bring women there. "I'll drive, and drop you back here after dinner." Hands low on his hips he studied her. "You game?"

"Let me get this straight," she said, fiddling with her braid. "You, Sam Cutter, are going to cook, without Cutter's takeout, pizza or TV dinners." Her brows arched. He nodded, and she almost smiled. "This I have to see."

"Great, but we'll need to stop at the grocery first."

"I wouldn't miss that for the world. I'll drive my own car, though. That way, this will feel more like dinner between friends and less like a date."

His sister lived a good ten miles from the studio, and it seemed silly to take two cars. But the last thing he wanted was a date. He nodded. "Agreed." He pushed open the door, ushering Amy out.

As she locked the studio door, she frowned. "This is a small town. Someone we know is bound to see us together. Think of the gossip and speculation that will cause."

Sam imagined people talking, then shrugged. "They're already talking, right? If we act like friends, they'll see that we are. That'll put an end to the rumors."

"I hope you're right."

For a Saturday afternoon the Forest Hills Grocery Store was packed. Wouldn't you know it, Amy thought. Any moment now, someone would spot her and Sam. Then the rumors would fly. How to explain—that Nina had cautioned her not to eat alone because the moon was in Cancer? That sounded totally wacky.

So what was she doing in the grocery store with her ex-husband? There was no simple answer to that, and this was no time to analyze her decision. Biting her lip she shot a brief, surreptitious glance at Sam. Darned if he didn't sense her gaze. He caught her eye and grinned. "Nervous?"

"A little," she admitted. Her heart tripped and pounded as it always did when he looked at her with that warm, you're-special expression. Lust, she told herself, and nothing more. He was not the right man for her. He never had been. And she wished she'd turned him down about dinner. *You still can,* a voice in her head said. "Maybe we should just go our separate ways."

"Look, we're friends on a mission to get what we need for dinner. That's nobody's business but ours," he said firmly. "So relax."

His conviction mollified her, at least enough to stay. "Okay."

"Good," he said. "Let's start in the meat department and work our way back." He grabbed a cart

and aimed it at the meat and poultry section, the far-
thest aisle away.

Amy followed alongside. Despite Sam's admon-
ishment to relax, she couldn't help feeling on edge.
As they wheeled forward she glanced at the men,
women and children clogging the aisles. Not a single familiar face—so far. She released a tight breath,
knowing she would not breathe freely until they
drove off.

At last they reached the meats. "Do you have
any preference on the steaks?" Sam asked.

Amy shook her head. He conferred with the
butcher, who seemed to know him, then selected
two large T-bones. Once they were wrapped and
priced, he dropped them into the cart. "Next, salad
fixings and potatoes," he said, aiming his cart toward the produce section.

The man certainly knew his way around the store.
Amy shook her head in wonder. "Do you realize
we've never grocery-shopped together? It was what
you called, 'the wife's job.'"

He gave a sheepish shrug as they rounded the
corner. "I didn't realize—"

"Sam," she interrupted in a low voice, grabbing
his arm. "There's Molly Andrews, one of my Rubies, and her mom, over by the lettuce." She didn't
want them to see her, and she tried to pull Sam toward another aisle. "Why don't we get a bottle of
wine first?"

But he planted his feet, and she couldn't budge him. "Amy, Amy," he said, shaking his head. "We're friends. That's nothing to hide."

It was too late, anyway, for Molly and her mother had spotted them. Molly, a slender, ponytailed blonde with long thin legs and naturally wide eyes gaped openly. Her mother, a plumper, darker-haired version, was more circumspect. Her jaw didn't drop but an interested gleam flashed in her eyes. She said something to her daughter and without taking their gazes from Amy and Sam, they steered their cart forward like detectives on a case.

As Sam took in the scene he inched fractionally closer to Amy. "Uh-oh, looks like trouble," he muttered.

"Told you so," Amy replied under her breath.

"Hi, Miss Parker," Molly said brightly. Tittering, she covered her mouth with her hand and glanced at Sam. "Hello, Mr. Cutter."

Sam nodded soberly, and Amy managed a tight smile. "Hello. Mrs. Andrews, have you and Mr. Cutter met?"

"No." Molly's mother smoothed her hair. Offering her hand, she shot him a warm, flirtatious smile. "Susan Andrews. Pleased to meet you."

"Sam Cutter," he said, seeming oblivious to her flustered reaction. Either he was unaware or so used to it he didn't notice.

The woman's speculative gaze darted from him

to Amy, and Amy could practically read her mind: *Amy and that gorgeous hunk, Sam Cutter, are together at the grocery. What a scoop! They must be dating.* She cringed at the thought. If people thought she and Sam were dating, who would ever ask her out? If she didn't date, she'd never meet the right man for her, the one who wanted to settle down and start a family. Which needed to happen fairly soon. She hastily sidestepped, putting a foot of space between her and Sam.

Mrs. Andrews took note, but the smug expression remained. "I am so sorry I had to reschedule this afternoon," she said without sounding one bit contrite.

"You weren't the only one," Amy replied. "In fact, only Sam showed up."

"Oh? That's odd." Mrs. Andrews suddenly grew interested in rearranging the contents of her cart. "Were you and Sam able to get anything done?"

Besides fight? Amy glanced at Sam, but his face was unreadable. She shrugged. "We managed."

"Actually, we finished a fair amount," he said.

Molly, who had stood silent and watchful, broke into nervous giggles.

"Stop it, Molly," her mother said with a stern shake of her head.

"I can't help it." The girl flushed. "*Miss Parker* is here with *Mr. Cutter*," she said, enunciating their names as if that explained the giggles and red face.

Amy felt her own face heat. She shifted uncomfortably beside Sam.

"Well, we do have to eat," he said. "We worked hard today and we're hungry."

That seemed to work. The girl nodded.

"So are we." Mrs. Andrews nudged her daughter. "Come on, Molly, let's finish up and get home." She winked. "You two enjoy yourselves tonight."

The gall! Amy lifted her head. "It's just a dinner between friends," she explained.

"Right," Sam added.

"Of course," the woman said, looking a lot like the proverbial cat who'd swallowed a canary.

Amy could practically see the wheels turning. Who would she call first with this juicy tidbit?

"Goodbye," Susan warbled.

"See you on Monday," Molly added as they pushed their cart away.

"That woman reminds me of a vulture," Sam said.

Amy nodded. "Don't say I didn't warn you. I don't want people to think we're dating."

"Neither do I. Come on, let's finish up and get out of here."

SAM FELT ODDLY ON EDGE as he ushered Amy into his sister's kitchen. What was the deal? They'd been alone together all afternoon, and this was no different. Amy seemed to sense the shift between them, too. She glanced nervously around while fiddling with her braid. "This is a beautiful place," she said at last.

Sam nodded as he placed the groceries on the counter. "Jeannie and Mike have done well."

Sam had, too, and he couldn't help wondering what Amy would think of his custom-built home on two wooded acres that overlooked a private lake at the back. Since he didn't intend to show it to Amy, he'd never know. He never brought dates there. And this was no date; it was dinner between friends.

So why was the very air thrumming with tension?

"I could use a glass of wine," he said, digging through the groceries for the merlot they'd purchased. He held up the bottle. "How about you?"

"Definitely," Amy said. "Where are the glasses?"

Sam opened the drawer where his sister stowed the corkscrew. "Over the buffet, in the dining room."

When Amy returned with two flutes, he filled both with the dark red liquid.

"To friendship," he said, lifting his glass.

"And an end to gossip," she added.

They clinked rims and sipped.

Amy smacked her lips in appreciation. "This is good stuff."

"I've learned a thing or two about wine."

She nodded. "Seems you've leaned a thing or two about a lot of subjects. I'm impressed, Sam."

He'd wanted her to be and couldn't hide his pleased grin. "I appreciate that."

She smiled back, and the tension faded. They sipped again. This was better.

"Make yourself at home," he said. He opened the back door, which led to a patio and secluded yard surrounded by an eight-foot high privacy fence. "I'll fire up the grill."

Minutes later, he returned to the kitchen, brushing his charcoal-blackened hands together. Amy was closing the oven door. "I washed the potatoes and put them in the oven."

Sam shot her a friendly frown as he washed his hands. "Hey, I thought I was supposed to cook."

"I can't just stand here doing nothing," Amy said. "Let me make the salad."

"As a symbol of our new relationship, we'll make it together," he said, drying his hands on a gingham towel. "By the time we're through, the coals should be ready." He eyed her magenta overalls and pale yellow T-shirt, which she'd managed to keep pristine after a day knee-deep in glue, paint and straw. "It'd be a shame to get those clothes dirty. You need an apron." He slid open the drawer in the bottom cupboard, grabbed a green bib apron and tossed it to her.

"Thanks." She slipped it over her head, then pulled her braid free. Reaching behind, she fumbled with the sash.

"I'll do that." Sam gestured her to turn around.

Careful not to stand too close, he reached for the sash. The loose end of her braid tickled his wrists, so he lifted the silken hair and dropped it over her shoulder. It was as soft and heavy as he remembered. Her faint, but fragrant vanilla scent filled his nostrils, and he felt the warmth from her body. Dear God, there was the sensitive place at crook of her neck. Kiss her there, and she'd murmur and lift her head to allow him more access. His groin stirred. The urge to touch his lips there, right now, grabbed hold of him. Unable to stop himself he lowered his head.

"Sam?" Amy asked, glancing over her shoulder. "What are you doing?"

"Nothing." Good thing she'd spoken, breaking the spell. Otherwise... He swallowed and kept his eyes on the sash while he looped the ends and pulled them snug. His knuckles grazed the soft flesh of her hips, and a tidal wave of desire crashed through him. Hands shaking, he jerked back.

They were friends. Nothing more, and that's how they both wanted it, he sternly reminded himself. "Better get started on the salad," he said gruffly, turning away to hide his arousal.

"Do you have a peeler for the carrots?" Amy asked.

Thankfully she seemed oblivious to his state. "In the top drawer," Sam said. He found the steamer, then brought it and the fresh broccoli to the sink. He then rinsed the stalks under ice cold water and added them to the steamer. He couldn't take a cold shower, but this was better than nothing. The steamer went on the stove. He'd turn on the burner just before he started the steaks. That way everything would be ready at the same time.

As soon as he moved from the sink, Amy took his place. She'd piled several kinds of salad vegetables on the counter. She selected a large carrot, cut off both ends, and washed it under a spray of water, rubbing the dirt with her fingers. The way she stroked that long, thick root remind Sam of the way she used to stroke him. God almighty. A fresh wave of desire flooded him, and the blood seemed to rush from his brain to his now-pulsing groin. He bit back a groan. How in the name of heaven was he going to survive this dinner?

She thrust the washed vegetable at him. "This is ready for chopping."

Sam moved to the cutting board a few feet away, paying close attention to his work. As long as he didn't watch Amy, he was fine.

Right, and he was a ballet dancer. He didn't have to look at her to want her.

She quickly washed mushrooms, radishes, tomatoes and a green pepper. Her stomach growled over the sound of the hissing water.

"Hungry?" Sam asked.

"Starved. Could I have a taste of that green pepper?"

Without thinking, he fed her a chunk. Her lips closed over his fingers for a brief moment. Sam felt the warmth and moisture of those lips clear to his groin. She was killing him. "Amy," he said on a ragged breath.

"Oh." Her brows arched. "Sorry." She backed away, but not before he saw the awareness that flared in her eyes.

So he wasn't the only one.

Sam cleared his throat. Pivoting away, he grabbed the steaks. "The coals should be ready."

Amy's face was flushed as she nodded. "I'll start the broccoli."

He couldn't get out the door fast enough. He lay the meat on the red-hot coals. The hiss of fat dripping released a billow of fragrant smoke. Squinting, he moved upwind. He could go inside now and finish chopping vegetables. But it was safer out here. He wanted Amy, wanted her so much. Sam clutched the barbecue tongs tightly in his fist. What kind of insanity had made him believe he could exchange wanting her for friendship?

The screen door scraped open, and Amy pushed through. "Sam," she said without meeting his eye.

"Yeah?" The waning sunlight dappled her face, catching the faint red wine stain of her lips and the fine smattering of freckles on her nose and cheeks.

"There are several salad dressings in the fridge," she said, at last looking at him. Her eyes, usually a sweet caramel color, had darkened. "What kind do you want?"

Unable to stop himself, he strode toward her. The tongs fell from his grasp, clattering onto the stone patio. He cupped her shoulder and backed her behind a lush rhododendron bush. "I want you."

Amy opened her mouth. He didn't wait for her to speak, just closed his eyes and kissed her.

Chapter Eight

AMY COULDN'T BELIEVE Sam was kissing her, couldn't believe how much she wanted him to keep right on doing it. But they were all wrong for each other. This had to stop. With every nerve in her body tense with longing, she placed her palms on his chest to push him away. Beneath her hands his heart thudded as hard as her own. "Don't," she protested weakly.

"Don't what?" he murmured against her mouth.

He broke the kiss to stare deeply into her eyes, probing as if he saw what was inside of her. He smelled of pine soap and smoke and his special Sam scent, and as he searched her very soul, his eyes, already filled with desire, seemed to smolder. Respondent need exploded in her, as if her body had been asleep for the past twelve years and had suddenly slammed into wakefulness. She couldn't look away any more than she could stem the hunger raging in her body. Amy forgot what she wanted to say.

"Never mind." She sighed, twining her arms around his neck. "Just kiss me again."

Sam made a sound of approval and offered a lazy, sexy smile. Then, still gazing into her eyes, he kissed her. Amy's eyelids drifted shut, and the world faded. There was only Sam, holding her close and kissing her with his fierce and possessive mouth. He nudged her lips open and plunged his tongue inside. He tasted of wine and Sam. He tasted of desire.

"Amy," he whispered, breaking the kiss to nibble his way down her neck.

She lifted and turned her head to allow him better access. He stopped at the sensitive crook of her neck. Her bones melted and she moaned, barely recognizing her own throaty sound.

"I've wanted to do that for so long," Sam said and she heard the smile in his voice.

Seeking contact with his body, she stood on her toes and pushed against him. Sam ground his hips against hers, his arousal evident even through the apron and her overalls. Frustration tore at her. She couldn't get close enough.

"Why don't you take off that bulky apron?" he suggested in sync with her very thoughts. He fumbled with the sash he had tied, undoing his work. In one motion, he pulled it over her head and flung it aside.

Emboldened by her desire and the heat in Sam's eyes, Amy smiled. "That's better, but not good enough." She reached for the hooks of her overalls. "I want to feel your hands on me. Touch me, Sam."

"I'd like that very much." He tugged at the straps and the bib dropped to her waist.

Amy pulled her T-shirt free. Sam lifted it over her head. He studied her lilac-color bra through hot, hooded eyes. "So you're still wearing pretty lingerie. I figured you might."

She arched one eyebrow. "You thought about my underwear?"

The corner of his mouth quirked. "You'd be surprised at what I've thought about."

"Such as?" she asked, teasing. But under the smile he knew she wanted to know.

"This." His hands shook as he unhooked the front clasp. Amy shrugged out of her bra, shivering in the cool evening air. "And looking at you." His eyes darkened as he stared at her breasts. "You're even more beautiful than I remembered."

Anticipation quivered through her. She closed her eyes for what seemed an eternity. At long last his hands were on her, his warm palms cupping her aching breasts. Her nipples were hard and sensitive, and Sam grazed them lightly with the pads of his thumbs, the way she liked. After all this time, he still remembered. His mouth soon replaced his hands, nipping and licking until pleasure flooded her senses and moisture dampened her panties. He was unfastening the button that kept her overalls from falling off. Soon he'd touch the aching place between her thighs. The very thought quickened her blood. Any minute now, she would climax, and she didn't want to do it alone. "Sam," she moaned, reaching for his swollen zipper, "please."

A sudden, shrill beep filled the air. "What's that?" Amy asked from a daze. She squinted at the masses of smoke coming from the grill and smelled the scent of burnt meat. Somehow, the sun had set and darkness had set in, and she could barely make out the charred lumps on the grill. "Oh, my gosh, the steaks."

Sam swore and released her. "There goes dinner," he muttered as he grabbed the tongs and tossed what was left of the steaks onto the grass. The hot meat sizzled in the evening dew. "All this smoke must have set off the alarm in the kitchen." He sped through the back door and disappeared.

Frustrated, embarrassed and astonished at her heated actions, Amy retrieved her scattered clothing, squinting through the darkness. Ignoring her bra, she tugged her T-shirt over her head and pushed her arms through the armholes. The cotton brushed her sensitized breasts, reminding her of what she and Sam had done. She bit her lip as she pulled her braid free. If not for the smoke alarm, she would have made love with Sam, the man who was all wrong for her. With a heavy heart she fastened the straps and shoved her bra into a pocket.

What had gotten into her? What had gotten into Sam? The alarm was still screeching, and she scowled in the direction of the kitchen. He'd started this whole mess by kissing her. Suddenly the noise stopped. In the beat of silence that followed, Amy silently admitted that she could have stopped him. Instead, she'd responded like a woman crazed with desire.

Crazy indeed, not to mention treading very dangerous waters. Angry at herself and also confused, she scooped up the apron and moved hesitantly toward the back door.

Two withered, overcooked baked potatoes sat on the stove. Black smoke billowed from the steamer, which Sam carried stiff-armed toward the sink. The unpleasant odor of burning broccoli filled the room. Amy wrinkled her nose. "Ugh."

"Amen for smoke alarms," he said. He set the pan in the sink and turned on the faucet, and a fresh jet of foul-smelling steam shot into the air. Sam jumped back. "So much for a home-cooked meal."

"I'm not hungry anymore, anyway," Amy said over the noise of rushing water.

Sam glanced over his shoulder at her. "We should talk," he said, shutting off the tap. In the moment of silence that followed he pivoted around. He cocked a hip against the counter, wiped his wet hands on his thighs and then hung his thumbs from his belt loops.

Amy couldn't help but glance at this crotch. He

was no longer aroused, but then, neither was she. She tugged her braid over her shoulder, the familiar weight like an anchor. "I'm sorry about dinner," she said. "But the truth is, what happened saved us from making a terrible mistake." Even though it had felt so right.

"I know." He gave a sober nod. "It shouldn't have happened." His gaze flickered to her breasts before he jerked his attention to her face. He cleared his throat. "Still, I can't say I'm sorry."

Neither am I, she thought. But she said, "Some things never change."

"That's a fact, and what just happened proves it. I guess this means we can't be platonic friends."

"I guess not."

His expression was fevered and intent, and she knew he remembered touching her and her frenzied response. Heaven help her, desire shivered up her spine. She folded her arms over her chest, compressed her lips and stared at the window behind Sam and above the sink. Darkness prevented her from seeing through the glass. Frowning she returned her focus to him. "This can't happen again."

"Tell me something I don't know." He scrubbed a weary hand over his face.

"From now on, we shouldn't be alone together. It's too dangerous."

"Agreed." He pushed away from the counter. "With that in mind, I'll see you to the door."

Amy sniffed the aroma of burnt broccoli and wrinkled her nose. "Don't you want help cleaning up?"

Sam shook his head. He grabbed Amy's purse from the chair in the breakfast nook and handed it to her carefully, as if he were afraid to touch her.

Hooking the strap over her shoulder she hurried through the door, held open by Sam. "Good night, Sam."

"See you around."

He stood in the threshold with his arms crossed and his face shadowed in the darkness. Just the same, Amy felt his gaze as she climbed into her car and started it. Self-conscious but wishing she weren't, she drove off without a glance in his direction.

As Sam drove toward the studio Monday afternoon, Mariah tilted her face toward him and pulled a quizzical frown. "Did you hear what I just said, Uncle Sam?"

"You need to stop at the library after rehearsal," he parroted absently. He'd left the office to pick up his niece from school thirty minutes ago. Since then, she'd carried on her usual one-sided, nonstop conversation. Sam had counted on her chatter to take his mind off his troubles—namely his unwanted fantasies about Amy. But he could hardly focus on anything the kid said.

He glanced out the side window. It had just stopped raining, and the trees lining the street dripped fat drops of water from their leafy branches like saturated sponges. His brain felt like that, over-loaded with thoughts of his ex-wife. He hadn't been so riveted on sex—in particular, sex with Amy—since high school. It had been two days since he'd lost his head and kissed her. Two days since he'd stroked her taut, rosy nipples and tasted her satiny skin. He couldn't get her out of his thoughts and he was going mad. Nothing, not even a Sunday trip to the zoo with Mariah and several cold showers, had distracted him.

As he neared the studio, an uncomfortable tension gripped him. He wished Mariah didn't have ballet today, because he sure as hell didn't want to see her teacher. Maybe he'd skip walking his niece inside. Jaw set, he slowed and signaled.

Mariah shot him a worried frown. "Are you mad, Uncle Sam?"

"'Course not," he said, forcing himself to relax.

"Then is something wrong?"

"Nope." He turned into the lot, slowing as he drove through a puddle. Several cars were parked near the door. Sam guessed they belonged to volunteers who hadn't shown up on Saturday. After his miserable weekend, he wished he'd backed out, too. His current predicament had started right here, in the back room of Amy's studio.

"Only seventeen days 'til the recital," Mariah said as he eased the Porsche into a slot. She'd been marking off the days on a calendar magnet attached to the kitchen refrigerator.

Amen to that. Sam nodded. "And a week from tomorrow your parents get back." Then he could stop driving his niece here and stop seeing Amy. Yes, he'd agreed to help out the night of the recital. But after that, he'd never see her again. He'd forget her and live his life without her, just as he'd done for the past twelve years. "I know they've missed you. Bet you'll be glad to get rid of me and have them back."

"Uh-huh." Suddenly silent, Amy toyed with the zipper of her tote bag.

Sam frowned. "Don't you want to see them?"

"Of course I do. But I'm having a great time with you, Uncle Sam."

"Back at ya, kid." He offered a fond smile. "And we can keep on having fun." *Just as long as I don't have to see Amy.*

"We'd better go in." Mariah opened her door, but when he didn't do the same, she glanced over her shoulder at him. Furrows lined her little brow. "Are you sure you're okay?"

"Yeah, I'm fine." If you didn't count his sexual frustration or his one-track mind. He opened his door. "Come on, let's go."

"Maybe you're getting sick," his niece suggested,

sounding like an adult. "It could be strep. Do you have a sore throat?"

Sam shook his head. Oh, he was sick, all right. Sick with lust for a woman he shouldn't want. As planned, he stopped at the door. "This is as far as I go today. I'll be back at five-thirty."

For once, Mariah didn't argue. "Okay."

As he reached for the door to usher her inside another car turned into the lot—a silver Mercedes coupe. "There's Janelle," Mariah said.

She was the daughter of Connie, who had morphed from flirt into rumormonger. Sam didn't want to run into her. But there was a man at the wheel. He squinted at the lightly tinted windows. "Who's driving?"

"Mr. Swanson, Janelle's dad. Do you want to meet him?"

Sam wanted only to leave, but his niece seemed eager for him to meet her friend's father. He shrugged. "Sure."

"Goodie. Hi, Janelle!" Mariah called out, running to meet her.

"Hi!" Janelle gamboled toward her friend, squealing with excitement. A tall, balding and mustached man about Sam's age trailed in her wake, clutching a grocery sack. Grabbing hands, the girls jumped up and down, as excited as kids on Christmas morning.

Janelle's father rolled his eyes. Sam shook his

head and grinned. "Sam Cutter," he said, offering his hand.

"Bob Swanson." He gave Sam's hand an enthusiastic shake. "My ex-wife told me she'd met you here. I've been following your career for years. Pleasure to meet you."

By the warmth of the man's greeting Sam figured Connie hadn't mentioned how she'd come on to him. He wondered what she'd said about him and Amy.

"I'm going inside, Daddy," Janelle called. "Don't forget to bring in the snack."

"I won't, baby. I'll be there in a sec."

"Bye, Uncle Sam," Mariah said.

Sam waved and the girls opened the door. Classical music spilled out, along with the sounds of Amy's voice, before the door closed.

"That Amy's a great teacher, with a sweet little body," Bob said, smacking his lips. "I hear you're dating her." He winked. "Lucky man."

Sam did not like the comment or the suggestive insinuation, and didn't try to hide his opinion. "You heard wrong," he said, shaking his head. "We're just friends." Which wasn't quite true, not after the other night. But he didn't correct his mistake.

Bob seemed taken aback by the menacing frown. "Just what kind of friends are you? Because you look like you'd deck me if I asked her out."

Sam realized his hands were clenched and his

jaw set. If Amy wanted to date this bozo, it was none of his concern. He uncurled his fists, schooled his expression to neutral and managed a causal shrug. "Ask away." He couldn't help adding, "She'll turn you down, though. She's too busy to date right now." *And you're not good enough for her.*

"Can't hurt to try," the balding man said. He pushed open the door. "Coming in?"

With Bob on the prowl, there was no way Sam could leave just yet. Besides, he wanted to gauge Amy's reaction to the slimeball. "For a minute."

He stopped inside the door, while Janelle's father swaggered forward like a man bent on a mission. Sam scowled at his back. There were no other adults around and he guessed the volunteers were working in the back room. Amy was at the barre, warming up with kids who seemed to hang on to her every word. Sam stood transfixed, watching her. Clad in a simple black leotard and pink tights, she pointed her toe and lifted one slender leg to the side. As always, her agility and grace awed him. Her arm swept a graceful arc as she raised it over her head. Sam caught his breath and forgot about leaving.

As if she felt his gaze, she stiffened and looked straight at him. Her mouth tightened, and though Sam stood too far away to see the nuances of her face, he knew there were tiny lines between her brows. Without stopping the warm-up, she widened her eyes. He had no choice but to nod a terse hello.

She dipped her head in acknowledgment, then turned away. She was acting as if nothing had happened the other night, as if they were strangers.

Which was for the best. After all, they'd agreed that those steamy kisses were wrong, and that they couldn't be friends. Even so, he'd expected a blush or some other sign that the other night had affected her as much as it had him. Her aloofness bothered him. Actually, it stung. Hands low on his hips, Sam narrowed his eyes at the scenario unfolding before him.

And tensed as Bob strolled right up to Amy. Sam's fingers twitched as he fought the urge to grab the man by the lapel of his expensive jacket and toss him out. If he made one rude comment to her…

To Sam's annoyance, she greeted Janelle's father with a bright smile as she accepted the grocery bag. Calling out instructions to her students, she left the barre to talk with him privately.

Sam stared darkly at the pair. The suave jerk was probably asking her out right now. By the pleased expression on her upturned face, she planned to accept.

Shock and misery rolled Sam's gut into an ugly knot. Scowling, he left the building.

Chapter Nine

AMY HAD JUST filled a colorful glass bowl with pretzels when her doorbell chimed Wednesday evening. No doubt Nina and Dani had arrived to address invitations for Nina's upcoming wedding. "Be right there," she called out.

On her way to the door she detoured past the mahogany dining-room table, where she set the pretzels beside a crystal carafe. The chandelier overhead winked warmly, and the jazz CD on the living room stereo provided lively and cheerful background music. Satisfied, she hurried through the small entry hall, catching the pleasant scent of fresh bouquet of lily of the valley she'd placed on the small table in the entry. She opened the solid wood door with a welcoming smile. "Come on in."

Her friends entered wearing wide grins. Amy hugged them one at a time and then stood back, beaming. "It's great to see you both. Seems like it's been ages."

"It has," Dani said as she hung her sweater on the antique brass coatrack near the door. "Can you believe this?" She gestured at her swelling belly.

"Wow," Amy said with an admiring shake of her head. "You're really getting big."

"And *I'm* getting desperate," said Nina, who despite her words seemed unperturbed. She held up a large pink shopping bag with rope handles. "In here are 183 invitations, and counting. We'll never get them done."

"Sure we will," Dani said.

Amy nodded. "With all three of us working, we'll finish in no time."

"I hope so, because these should have been mailed yesterday."

"Did you bring the mailing lists?" Amy asked.

Nina nodded. "I divided it into three sections, one for each of us, just like you suggested. I also brought calligraphy pens and stamps."

"Then what are we waiting for? I think the dining room table will work best." Amy turned and led the way.

"Look at that—a crystal carafe and matching glasses," Nina said. She sniffed appreciatively. "And fresh tulips and lilacs on the buffet. You weren't supposed to go to any trouble."

"Other than stopping at the store for pretzels, I didn't," Amy said.

"Putting out flowers, and using the fancy crystal

just for us…but then, you always go the extra mile. That's part of what makes you so special."

Amy acknowledged the compliment with a pleased smile. "Thank you." She gestured them to sit at one end of the table. When everyone was settled, she filled the wine flutes with sparkling cider owing to Dani's pregnancy.

Each woman lifted her glass. "To getting this job done tonight," Nina said.

They clinked rims and sipped. Amy passed the pretzels. Then Dani doled out the supplies, and they settled down to work and conversation.

"How are the wedding plans coming along?" Amy asked as she penned the first address.

Nina looked up from the envelope in front of her. "Things are progressing nicely. We've picked the cake and decided on the rest of the food. Last week I ordered the flowers. Ben is meeting with the band to finalize the particulars. They specialize in oldies and have promised us a night of dancing and fun. This is going to be a dynamite celebration." She seemed to glow as she regaled them with details.

Amy stemmed a pang of envy. How wonderful to be in love, and to be loved in return. For some reason she thought of Sam. Her heart lifted and fluttered. Probably heartburn, she told herself. He was the wrong man for her, and they both knew it. "It all sounds fabulous," she sighed.

Dani nodded. "It's better than fabulous. But

everything seems to happen in a blink, so enjoy each moment, Nina." She looked wistful. "Seems like yesterday that Russ and I got married. Now we're into our third year, and here I am, pregnant." Radiating happiness, she laid a palm over her belly.

For several minutes, Amy and her friends worked in silence, each lost in her own thoughts. Amy could only imagine how Dani felt. She fervently hoped that in the not-too-distant future she, too, would experience the joys of marriage and impending motherhood. Her Mr. Right was out there. She just had to find him.

"How's the recital coming along?" Dani asked.

"Everyone who cancelled on Saturday showed up during the week. The sets and invitations are finally done, and the costumes made. The kids are hard at work memorizing their parts." Amy's friends had supported her from the beginning, and she filled them in on the details she knew they enjoyed hearing about. Not every detail, though. She was determined to steer clear of certain subjects, namely Sam Cutter.

Nina lifted her pen from an envelope to glance sharply at Dani. "She's not going to tell us," she said as if she'd read Amy's thoughts.

Dani, too, stopped writing. Both women stared questioningly at Amy.

Had they somehow guessed about her and Sam? Could they see the pitiful truth in her face—that ever since sharing those dangerous kisses she ached for more, that she couldn't seem to stop thinking about him? But due to a tacit agreement—that the less contact between them, the better—she'd only seen Sam once, when he dropped off Mariah on Monday. They hadn't spoken, had barely acknowledged each other before he'd left. She hadn't seen him since, which was for the best. Nor had she mentioned him to anyone. She felt certain he had been equally close mouthed. Her friends couldn't know.

She glanced from Dani to Nina, noting the identical gleams of interest in their eyes. To Amy's horror her cheeks warmed. She grabbed an invitation and pretended to study the mailing list. "There's nothing to say," she told them before clamping her lips shut.

"You're going out with Bob Swanson after the recital," Dani said. "That's not 'nothing,' Amy."

So they didn't know about her and Sam. Amy couldn't stem her relief. "He asked and I said yes." At her friends' dismayed looks, she added, "I meant to tell you, but it slipped my mind." Which it had. The truth was, she wasn't interested in Bob. But she had to start somewhere. And if she wanted to find a husband, she couldn't turn down the opportunity to get to know the eligible bachelor. Who knew, she just might end up liking him.

"Bob's got a reputation for fooling around with several women at the same time. He fooled around on Connie. That's why she divorced him. He's supposed to be a fast mover, too."

Amy absorbed the information with a nod. "I hadn't heard that. Thanks for alerting me."

Nina sealed the invitation she'd just addressed. She added it to the growing pile of mail. "I'll bet Sam went ballistic when he heard."

As far as Amy knew, Sam hadn't heard. Not that it mattered. "Why should he mind? Whom I choose to date is none of his business."

Dani's jaw dropped and Nina snorted. "Do we look stupid?" she asked.

"Of course not! But I'm telling you, there is nothing going on between Sam and me."

"Right," Dani said, "and I'm not carrying twins. I know you, and I know when you're messing with the truth. Besides, Susan Andrews saw you with Sam last Saturday at the grocery."

"You didn't tell us. That hurts." Nina gave her head a sad shake. "This is us, Nina and Dani. Your best friends. We've never had secrets from each other. You can't leave us in the dark and expect us to hear about your life from someone else. Think how you'd feel if we treated you that way."

They were right, Amy acknowledged. The three of them had always shared their concerns, doubts and insights with each other. "I apologize." She capped her pen, bit her lip and gave in. "What happened is, after the work party last Saturday, the one where everybody but Sam cancelled, he offered to cook me dinner."

"*Sam* cooked you dinner?" Nina asked, looking incredulous.

Amy nodded. "Well, you told me not to eat alone."

"So Sam cooks. My, my, how times do change," Dani said. She leaned forward, frowning when her belly limited the movement. "Did he take you to his place?"

Amy knocked the knowing look from her friend's face with a stern frown. "Is it any wonder I didn't tell you? Stop looking at me like that," she chided. "This wasn't a date, just a dinner between friends. I drove myself. We met at his sister's house, where he's staying while Mariah's parents are on that cruise."

"So his niece was with you?" Nina asked, looking disheartened.

"No, she went to a friend's."

"Aha." Nina gave a brief nod. "And?"

Amy fiddled with the list and stewed over what to say. True, these were her best friends, the women she trusted more than anything. Yet how could she tell them about those kisses and more, about the passion so intoxicating that the food had burned to a crisp right under her and Sam's noses? Even thinking about his avid kisses and clever fingers, and the intense pleasure generated by the man's tongue, quickened her pulse.

She stared at the flocked wallpaper a moment, corralling her emotions before she spoke. "That's private," she said. Dani opened her mouth and Nina made a sound, but Amy hurried on before either spoke. "Let's just say, we never did eat. We agreed that we couldn't be friends and decided to go our separate ways."

Dani and Nina exchanged sad looks. "How disappointing," Nina said.

Amy agreed, but there wasn't much to be done about it. She and Sam were wrong for each other, and nothing could change that. Sad, but true. Emptiness filled the hollow space in her chest, but she ignored it. She wasn't about to own up to her feelings. Not even to her best friends.

FRESH FROM A BUBBLE BATH and wrapped in her apricot-colored terry-cloth robe, Amy sank onto her comfortable chintz sofa. She rarely indulged in long baths on Saturday nights, but with the recital in two weeks she'd rehearsed the kids long and hard today. She'd needed a relaxing, hot soak to ease her hip and drain away the tension. Yawning, she turned on the television and flipped through the channels. Not much on tonight. She considered falling into bed for the night but it was only eight, way too early. And totally pathetic. She glanced at a new chick-lit novel on the coffee table, but she was too tired to read and, thanks to Sam, too restless to concentrate.

At the very thought of the man, she shifted irritably, clicked off the television and tossed aside the remote. She hadn't seen him since Monday afternoon, when they'd exchanged uncomfortable nods. That had been the extent of their meeting. Then, just before rehearsals ended late this afternoon, Sam had shown up for Mariah, striding into the studio with the power and strength of a man who knew what he wanted and went after it. As always, Amy's breath had caught and her heart seemed to leap with gladness. Unwanted desire washed over her, and she forgot that they were barely speaking. Like a moth drawn to a flame she turned toward him. His dark frown snapped her back to reality.

Amy had matched his expression with a stern look of her own. His eyes had flashed and narrowed, giving her the distinct impression his bad mood was her fault. Her stomach had clenched with guilt and worry, and for a moment she'd felt just as she had so often during their marriage: that Sam's moods depended on her. But she was no longer a naive young girl and they were no longer married. She was not responsible for Sam or his attitude. Her distress gave way to a defensive, raised chin and a confrontational glare.

He'd motioned her to the office, out of earshot of her curious students. Then, arms folded, he'd grilled her. "Why are you going out with Bob Swanson?"

The unexpected question had caught her off guard, and her jaw had dropped. "What?"

"He's not right for you. I've checked him out. The man is a total womanizer."

Nina and Dani had told her the same thing. Coming from Sam, the information seemed too much like a need to control. "You checked him out?" she sputtered, growing angrier by the moment. "I don't need your protection, Sam. In case you haven't noticed, I'm a grown woman. I can take care of myself."

"Do a friend a favor and look what happens?" he muttered.

"We aren't friends, remember? We tried that and it doesn't work."

She had uttered the truth and they both knew it. Yet the moment the words left her lips, she wanted to call them back, for Sam had reeled as if she'd slapped him. His mouth compressed into a thin line. Then he gave a terse nod. Without another word, he pivoted away and strode out of the office. His back to her, he'd quickly collected his niece and several other girls and hurried them out.

Since then, Amy had felt restless, bewildered and out of sorts. She thought about apologizing, but no. Sam should apologize. This fight had been his fault. If he hadn't meddled in her business… But rationalizations didn't help. Somehow she felt responsible for what had happened this afternoon. And why must she rehash the scene yet again? Unable to sit still any longer, she rose. Maybe she'd get dressed and go to a movie.

The doorbell chimed. Who could that be? Amy wasn't expecting anyone. She frowned, tightening the sash of her robe on the way to the door. She flipped on the porch light and peered through the peephole. Her frown turned to shock when she saw who stood there. *Sam.* She unlocked the door and opened it. Several moments passed before she found her voice. "What are you doing here?"

"I need to tell you something," he said. Despite the cool spring night, he wore a black T-shirt and no jacket. In the yellow porch light, his eyes were unreadable and his face shadowed. His gaze darted over her, making her acutely aware of her robe, bare legs and bare feet. And that she was naked underneath. Not that he could tell.

She hooked her right foot, the one with the biggest callus, behind her left ankle. That made her hip hurt, and she rubbed it absently. "Oh?"

He glanced over her shoulder, into the house. Amy thought about inviting him in, but decided against that. It was too dangerous. Last time they'd been alone, they'd nearly made love. Grasping the door, she nodded. "I'm listening."

Sam shifted from one foot to the other, then shoved his hands into the pockets of his jeans. "I, uh—" Pausing, he cleared his throat. "About this afternoon and what I said. It's your life and I shouldn't have interfered."

"No, you shouldn't have." She started to fold her

arms over her chest but remembered her robe, which liked to gape open. Grabbing the lapels she pulled them together.

"You're right, you're a grown woman—a strong, beautiful woman," he said as his gaze again flickered over her. "Perfectly able to make your own decisions." He looked deeply into her eyes. "I'm sorry I tried to tell you what to do."

The words and Sam's earnest expression went straight to her heart. "I shouldn't have overreacted," she said. "I know you meant well. I accept your apology."

He peered at her as if evaluating her words. Then the air whooshed from his lungs, as if he'd been holding his breath. "Good." After a moment, he scrubbed the back of his neck and shifted again. "I accomplished what I came here for. I'll leave you alone now."

"Would you like to come in?" she blurted out. Immediately she wanted to recall the offer, but it was too late. "Unless you have to pick up Mariah?" she asked hopefully.

Sam shook his head. "She's at a slumber party." He shrugged. "I can come in."

He stepped into the entry, pausing to wipe his sneaker-clad feet on the throw rug. He was a big man, and he filled a good bit of the small space. His gaze roamed the living room, from the coved stucco ceilings and plate railings to the thick area rugs atop the polished hardwood floor. "Nice place," he said with admiration. "Looks real homey. But then, you always were good at that."

The compliment pleased her. "Thanks," she said. Good manners compelled her to offer him a seat and refreshment. "Would you like a soft drink or a glass of wine?"

"Nothing, thanks." He sank onto the couch, the most comfortable piece of furniture in the room, and exactly where Amy wanted to sit.

She considered asking him to scoot over, but quickly nixed that idea. Despite their strained relationship, the undercurrent of sexual awareness between them seemed as strong as ever. For that reason, she took the staid Queen Anne chair across the coffee table. Holding her lapels securely closed and keeping her knees tightly together, she sat down.

In the uncomfortable silence that followed, she racked her brain for something to talk about. Meanwhile, hands on his thighs, Sam regarded her openly. His attention made her self-conscious. She wished she'd put off the bath and had stayed in her street clothes. Instead, here she was with no makeup, in a robe and nothing underneath. At least it was a thick robe. There was no way for Sam to know she was naked under it.

Suddenly she was aware of the nubby terry cloth as it brushed her nipples. She felt them stiffen. Embarrassed, she pretended to brush a fleck of something from her sleeve. She studied Sam from lowered lids. With his snug jeans and relaxed posture, she couldn't help a glance at the healthy bulge between his legs. She imagined herself boldly moving to the sofa, touching him there. He would groan and fling her against the cushions, and...

Amy swallowed. Antsy with yearning, she shifted. He hadn't even moved and she wanted him. Oh, why had she invited him in? Thank heavens he couldn't read her mind.

At last, Sam broke the silence. "It's been one hell of a week."

Glad for something to talk about, Amy nodded sympathetically. "Tell me about it. Exactly two weeks from tonight, my students will dance in their very first recital. You can't imagine how—"

"I'm not talking about work," he interrupted. "I'm talking about us." Heat flared in his eyes.

"Oh." Maybe he *had* read her mind. And maybe he should leave. Nervously, she fiddled with the sash of her robe. "Listen, Sam—"

"Amy, I—" he said at the same time.

The both stopped. "Go ahead," Sam said.

"After you."

Sam nodded. He glanced at the Tiffany-style light fixture and pulled on the neck of his shirt as if it were too tight. Finally he let out a breath and looked straight at her. "I don't know how to say this so I'll just say it straight. This…thing…between us is so strong, it's killing me. I thought the feelings would go away if we didn't see each other, so I've kept my distance all week. But that hasn't helped. Neither have cold showers or long runs." His anguished gazed sought hers. "I can't stop thinking about you or wanting you."

His words could have come from her own mouth. Her heart thudded in her chest. In a quandary over what to say, Amy chewed her lower lip. "Me, too," she admitted at last.

"What are we going to do about it?" Sam asked.

"Don't you remember? We decided to avoid each other."

"Yet here we are, alone in your living room." He laughed without humor. "Obviously we didn't follow our own advice." He scrubbed a hand over his face. "The truth is, I need to make love with you." He shot her a bold, sexy look. "And I think you need the same thing."

"What?" she gasped. "Is this why you're here? Because you want sex?"

He started to shake his head, then his brow furrowed as he thought about that. "Considering that I shoved a handful of condoms in my pocket before I left home, maybe it is." The corner of his mouth quirked. "All I know is, we have to move past this fixation with each other. That won't happen until we get this passion out of our systems. Making love is the only way I can think of to do that." He raised one brow. "Unless you have a better idea?"

Against her better judgment she considered the suggestion. Her rational mind knew that making love with Sam was a bad idea, yet her body yearned for him. "No." Her insides were in turmoil, and she frowned. "We tried that with kisses, and it only made things worse."

"Because kisses weren't enough," he said, shooting a hot look at her mouth.

"What makes you think making love once will end this craziness between us?"

Sam rubbed his chin. "It'll have to. I don't want to fall into old habits and patterns." Pain registered in his eyes. "It hurts too much when it's over."

"It certainly does," Amy added softly. Since they were speaking openly, she voiced her biggest worry. "What if we fall in love again?"

"We won't," he assured her with conviction. "Once was enough for me. And we both agree that I'm the wrong man for you." He cast a clear-eyed yet heated gaze at her. "Let's end this torture tonight. Make love with me, Amy."

She could no more turn him down than she could stop breathing. With the decision made, every nerve in her body jumped to life. Swallowing audibly around her suddenly dry throat, she nodded.

Holding her gaze, Sam stood. He moved purposefully toward her.

She rose on legs that trembled and met him halfway.

There was no turning back.

Chapter Ten

SAM'S HEART POUNDED in his chest as he pulled Amy into his arms. He was already hard with need. She did that to him, and she didn't even realize it. The way she angled her chin. Her laugh when she bit her lip. Executing a dance step, or arguing with him. No matter what she did, he wanted her. He was crazy in lust. And finally, finally he was going to get her out of his system. Eager to kiss her he tipped up her chin. Her sober expression stopped him.

"Having second thoughts?" he asked, praying she hadn't changed her mind. If she turned him down now, he'd never be the same.

"No," she said, to his relief. "It's just, suddenly I'm a little nervous."

That he could handle. "Don't be." He kissed the tip of her nose. She smelled clean and fresh with a hint of vanilla. "Why don't I undo your braid, the way I used to?"

"Okay, but I should do yours first."

Sam nodded and turned his back. She tugged at the elastic holding his hair back. An instant later his hair fell loose, hanging just short of his shoulders. He pivoted around. Standing on her toes, Amy tucked it behind his ears. "There," she said, still sounding nervous.

"Thanks." Sam smiled. "Your turn."

She turned away, showing her back. He lifted the thick rope of hair from her back and fumbled with the elastic band at the end. He dropped it into the pocket of her robe, then spent a moment kneading her sore hip.

"Ah," she sighed.

Under the soft flesh on her hips, he felt the lean muscle, tight and knotted. He worked a few minutes in silence. "How's the pain now?"

"What pain?"

Sam grinned. "Back to your hair."

Nodding, she bowed her head. He unraveled the ropes of her braid. Silken strands of light brown hair tickled his wrist and caught between his fingers. When he reached the base of her skull he gently raked his fingers through her hair until it rippled down her back. "All done," he said. Then, just like he used to, he lifted the hair from her neck, bent down and kissed her nape.

A tremor shook through her. It had been a long time, but Sam knew what that meant. She wanted him. His own hands shook as he turned her to face him.

Her eyes were closed, and her dark lashes swept softly against her cheeks. An odd, tender feeling filled his chest, surprising given the force of his desire. Awed at the depth of emotion churning within, he cupped her upturned face and reverently kissed each eyelid. He planted a light kiss on the tip of her nose. Then he gently brushed her lips in a kiss so sweet that his knees threatened to give out. "Feeling better now?" he murmured against her lips.

Her eyes opened part way. They were dark and hot with desire. "Much better," she whispered, wrapping her arms around his neck. She stretched up on her toes, pressed her body close, and kissed him with an eagerness that broadsided him.

His body caught fire. Nudging her lips open, he deepened the kiss. Her tongue tangled wildly with his. Tenderness forgotten, he grasped her behind and ground his hips against hers. "I want you, Amy. Feel how much."

"I want you, too, Sam," she murmured in a throaty, seductive voice. "We should go upstairs, to my bedroom."

"Uh-huh," he replied, but he didn't think he could make it that far. He nuzzled the sensitive place where her neck met her shoulder. Needing to touch her, he slipped his hand inside her robe. Dear God, she was naked. Her nipple was hard and erect and… Blood roared in his ears. He wanted her here, now. But she wasn't ready. Groaning, he forced himself to slow down. Remembering what she liked, he lightly pinched her nipple.

She gasped. "Then again, who needs a bed?"

"I want to taste you, all over," he growled. Grabbing her hand, he dragged her to the couch, unfastening the sash of her robe on the way.

"Not the sofa," she said breathlessly. "It's too short for you." She tugged on his hand, pulling him onto the thick rug.

Sam's mouth quirked. "You always were good at logistics."

"I know."

Smiling, she lay back. He plucked a throw pillow from the couch and propped it under her head. Quickly, he toed off his sneakers, then tugged off his T-shirt and threw it aside. When he turned to her she'd opened her robe, revealing her taut dancer's body. Sam gazed in admiration at her pale skin and the small but perfect breasts. Her waist was slender and supple. He glanced at the thatch of light brown hair at the apex of her thighs and swallowed. "You are so beautiful," he murmured. Leaning down he teased her nipples with his thumbs.

Shivering, she arched her back. "Oh, Sam. That feels…so good."

Giving her pleasure aroused him even more. He lay down beside her. "Bet you still like this, too." Taking a nipple in his mouth, he swirled his tongue over the sensitive peak. Then suckled gently.

Amy moaned. "You bet right."

Threading her hands through his hair, she urged him closer while he thoroughly enjoyed each breast. Awash in the pleasure of tasting her, he trailed open-mouth kisses down the soft skin of her stomach. Her legs parted. He kissed her tender inner thigh, felt her tense as he neared her most sensitive place.

She was wet and musky with her woman's scent. Sam flicked his tongue. Groaning, she clamped her hands onto his ears. Still tonguing her, he inserted two fingers inside her slick, hot passage. Instantly she cried out and convulsed around him.

Her climax was such a turn-on, he nearly came with her. When she at last sighed and went slack, he nuzzled her stomach. Then, propped on his forearm, he kissed her lips.

"That was...amazing," she said.

Her face and chest were flushed and her eyes dark and luminous with arousal. He smiled at her and she smiled back. "You're pretty amazing, yourself."

"Now, I want to touch you." She pushed him onto his back. Still smiling, she stroked his chest and pulled gently on his nipples the way he liked. *She remembers,* he noted through a haze of desire.

Her hand trailed the fine line of hair down his belly, all the way to his belt. Sam tensed. Through slitted eyes, he watched her unfasten the buckle. She undid the button at the top of his fly. Then she reached for his strained zipper.

The instant she brushed him, he sucked in a tortured breath, circled her wrist and lifted her hand. "Don't, or I'll explode."

"I was hoping you'd do that inside of me."

Despite their earlier conversation and the fire raging in his blood, he had to ask. "Are you sure about this?"

"Yes," she replied without hesitation.

Her certainty erased the last of his doubts. He struggled to his feet, digging into his hip pocket where he'd stashed a quantity of condoms. He extracted one, kicking off his jeans at the same time. His Jockeys and his socks followed. With his teeth, he tore open the foil packet. Sheathing himself, he joined Amy, who had spread the robe under herself like a blanket. Her expression full of longing, she reached for him.

He kissed her as he covered her with his body. Her legs parted and she tilted up her hips. Sam let out a growl and slowly entered her. She was hot, tight and wet. "Oh, God," he moaned. "I don't think I can hold back."

Amy gripped his hips with her thighs, the way he'd dreamed of for so long. "I don't want you to," she whispered. "Let go, Sam."

He plunged deep, eased out and plunged again. And again. Each time, the coil of tension tightened between them. Suddenly, Amy released a funny, whimpering sound. Clutching his waist, she convulsed around him. An instant later, the world tilted and Sam joined her.

When his breathing slowed and his sanity returned, she was nestled against his side. Sam felt fantastic. Sex with Amy was even better than he remembered. He kissed the top of her head. "Wow," he said, propping himself on his forearm.

She wore a languid, satisfied expression. "You said it," she murmured drowsily. "That was wonderful."

"The best."

"Can you reach the afghan on the arm of the sofa, and maybe flip off the lights?"

"On the way back from the bathroom. Where is it?"

"Down the hall, first door on your left," she said, sounding drowsy.

Within moments, Sam was headed again for the living room, his mind whirling. They'd both gotten what they wanted: red-hot, satisfying sex. Briefly, he thought about heading home. Until he saw Amy. Wrapped in her robe on the rug, she smiled at him. Her lips were red and slightly swollen, and her face and neck still wore the rosy flush of desire. She'd never looked more beautiful. His heart swelling with emotion, Sam smiled back. Leaving now might seem rude, and besides, he wasn't ready to go just yet. He'd stay a while longer. He grabbed the afghan, then found and flipped off the light switch.

He returned to his place beside her, shook the blanket over them, and again drew her close. "Miss me?"

"I sure did." Amy snuggled against his side, resting her head on his chest. "I'm glad you're back."

"Me, too," Sam replied. The thick rug was reasonably comfortable, and the woman against his side warm and soft. He shut his eyes and slept.

Sometime later, a clock chimed softly, waking him. What time was it? He pushed the light on his watch and squinted at the dial. Not quite midnight. He should leave, he thought, idly stroking Amy's hip, the side of her breast, her shoulder.

She murmured in her sleep, then turned toward him. Her fingertips brushed across his groin before settling on his belly. Desire licked through him, and just like that, he was rock-hard. Sam scrubbed a hand over his face and swore silently.

His plan had seemed so logical: make love with Amy and satisfy his desire for good. Too bad things had backfired. Instead of getting Amy out of his system, he only wanted her more.

AMY AWAKENED SLOWLY. Though it was dark, she knew where she was—cuddled up with Sam on the living room floor. Against her better judgment she'd made love with him. She tried to summon up panic or at least a trace of worry, but with her head pillowed on his warm, solid chest and his arm anchoring her close, it was difficult to chide herself about her foolish behavior. She drew in a slow, deep breath, and the familiar smells of pine-scented soap and Sam's unique scent filled her senses. He smelled so good, and this felt so right.

Longing flared in her. She knew she shouldn't want Sam again. But she did, too much to pretend otherwise. She flicked her tongue across his nipple, then flung her thigh over his hips. He was aroused. A low groan rumbled in his chest, and then she was flat on her back, her hands pinned to the floor by his. His shadowed face loomed inches above hers, so close that they shared the same breath. He liked to wake up making love, she remembered. So did she. Desire flamed through her. She wanted him so much. But they'd agreed to make love once and only once.

"We shouldn't," she said.

"You're right. Unfortunately we have a problem." He sounded strained, as if his teeth were gritted. "I still want you." He stopped talking to kiss the tender underside of her arm. "And you still want me."

It was pointless to argue when her bones had just melted. "What should we do?" she asked on a shuddering breath of need.

"Change the rules," he said, shifting closer. "Maybe we need one, full night of making love."

With Sam so close and her need so urgent, it was hard to think. "That sounds like an excellent idea," she managed.

He blew out a huge breath. "I'm glad you agree. But when morning comes, we stop. For good."

"For good," she repeated.

"I'll find the condoms." He released her hands. "Don't go away," he said, kissing her lips lightly.

She heard rustling as he searched for his clothes. "Just how many condoms did you bring with you tonight?" she asked.

"A handful," he said. He made a satisfied sound and ripped open a packet.

Despite her desire, his statement bothered her. Her mouth tightened. "So you didn't just stop by to apologize. You knew you'd get 'lucky' tonight. You planned out this whole thing, didn't you?"

"Not exactly. But I was a Boy Scout, remember? I'm always prepared." He dropped down beside her and gave her a long, passionate kiss. "Aren't you glad?" he whispered, nuzzling her breasts.

Gasping, she arched her back. Preoccupied as she was, she couldn't find fault with his reasoning, nor did she want to. "Oh, yes."

His clever fingers found the aching bud between her legs. "You want to go upstairs, to your bed?"

"I can't wait that long," she said breathlessly.

"Next time, then," he said.

WHEN AMY AWOKE Sunday morning, she was on her side, facing the bedroom window. Sam lay curled around her, spoon-style. He was still asleep, she knew by the even sound of his breathing. Unwilling to wake him just yet, she remained motionless. She opened her eyes to a bedroom bright with daylight. The yellow lace curtains provided scant protection from the morning sun. She should have closed the blinds. But by the time she and Sam had made it upstairs, she'd been too preoccupied with him to remember.

They'd made love all night long—passionate love tempered with tenderness and once, when they were both panting with need, desperately fast. They'd tasted every inch of each other's bodies with wild abandon. Just before dawn, they'd used up the last of the condoms. Exhausted, they'd fallen asleep.

And now it was over.

She would never again make love with Sam. Last night they'd agreed—one night and only one night. A smart decision, but at the moment, Amy felt anything but smart. She bit her lip.

Unfortunately, she'd screwed up. Sometime during the night she'd lost her heart to him. She'd fallen in love all over again. No, that wasn't quite true. She'd never stopped loving Sam. Only she'd refused to admit it to herself. But now she could no longer hide the truth.

What in the world had possessed her to spend the night in his arms? He wasn't right for her, and she wasn't right for him. They were too different. They didn't want the same things. Good, logical reasons for not losing her heart. Trouble was, her heart didn't care a whit about logic.

No longer able to lie still, she tried to scoot away. Sam's arms tightened around her.

"Rise and shine," she prodded brightly as she managed to slip from his grasp.

He released her, cracked open one eye and groaned. "What time is it?"

Suddenly shy of her nudity despite what they'd done to each other during the night, she sat up, pulling the patchwork quilt with her. She glanced at the clock on the bedside table. "Almost nine."

Sam swore. "I meant to sneak out early this morning, before any nosy neighbors saw my car out front."

"Too late to worry about that now," Amy said. "Besides, it's Sunday. People sleep in. Maybe no one noticed."

"In Forest Hills? Fat chance. Well, we're adults. What we do is nobody's business but our own." He rolled onto his back and sat up beside her. The sheet bunched around his hips, leaving his chest gloriously bare.

"I couldn't agree more." Even now she wanted to run her hands over his skin, feel his muscles quiver as her fingers traced a path to his groin... Jerking her gaze up, she pinned her attention to his morning beard. He needed a shave. "What time are you supposed to pick up Mariah?"

"At ten." He studied her openly. "You okay?"

"A little tired, and maybe a little sore. Aside from that, fine." If you didn't count the ache in her chest. She forced a smile. "What about you?"

"The same. I really enjoyed last night."

"Me, too."

They shared a warm look, and Sam offered a sexy, crooked grin that melted her heart. But this was no time for foolishness. She managed a casual shrug. "At last, we're out of each other's systems. Thank goodness, huh?"

"Right." His grin slipped as he nodded several times.

A sudden, uncomfortable silence sprang between them, dispelling the heated intimacy of the night before.

Searching her mind for something to say, Amy angled her chin toward the clock. "It's almost time to pick up your niece—"

"I should get moving—" Sam said at the same moment. He swung his legs over the bed, then glanced over his shoulder at her. "Mind if I shower here? Or a bath, if you have only the tub."

"There's a shower, in the guest bedroom down the hall, and fresh bath towels hanging. The soap and shampoo are in the medicine cabinet."

"Thanks."

Tossing back the covers he rose, unselfconscious as he padded across her bedroom naked. He'd always been like that, a man comfortable with his body. Amy gave him an admiring glance. He was beautiful and strong, but not overly muscular. And she would never again smooth her palms down his long, straight back or feel his heartbeat against her breasts. The knowledge made her feel empty and alone.

She swallowed her sadness and pinned a smile on her face until she heard the guest bathroom door close. Then she moved mechanically into her own bathroom for a quick bath. When the water rushed loudly into the tub, she let the tears flow.

Chapter Eleven

SAM WAS NOT happy, he acknowledged as he toweled dry after his shower. He thought he might be falling for Amy all over again. Not smart. Loving her meant pain, and he did not want to experience that kind of misery ever again. Besides, she was over him now. She'd said as much a little while ago. *"At last we're out of each other's systems."* He frowned, remembering.

He'd left his clothes downstairs, so he wrapped the towel around his waist and strode toward the staircase. He didn't fault Amy for what she'd said, since the whole reason for making love was to get over their mutual physical need.

It just hadn't happened for him.

On the way to the stairs he passed her bedroom. She was no longer there, but the bed was a rumpled mess, a testament to the night he'd never forget. The sex between them had been better than he'd remembered, the best sex of his entire life. He'd never made love so many times in one night and with such intensity, never forgotten where he ended and his partner began. But it was over now, he grimly reminded himself.

He moved silently down the carpeted steps. His clothes and socks lay neatly folded beside his sneakers. He retrieved them and dressed quickly. The throw pillow and afghan were back on the sofa. She'd straightened up as if nothing had happened.

Which underlined her statement earlier. She really *was* over him. Sam envied her. He stared at the rug where plenty had happened.

They'd made love twice here before moving upstairs. Then they'd moved to Amy's clawfoot tub for a wet and wild bath. After that, several more times in her bed. Yet after all that loving, crazy as it was, he still wanted her—even more than before. He gave his head a firm shake. Amy had taken their agreement to heart, and so would he. There would be no more sex with her, and if he knew what was good for him, he'd stop wanting her right now. Resolute, he nodded at the condom wrappers in the waste basket. Goodbye, wrappers, and goodbye misguided lust.

Time to leave. He knew exactly where Amy was by the rich aroma of fresh-brewed coffee. Following the scent, he found the kitchen.

She was standing before the coffee maker at a white-and-blue tiled counter, staring out the window that overlooked the postage-stamp-size backyard. Her back was to Sam, and she didn't seem to know he was there. He took advantage of that to study her for a moment, knowing he'd likely never see her again like this—never again, period, after the recital the week after next. She'd re-braided her hair and the ends were damp, as if she'd just bathed. She'd dressed in loose, faded jeans and a heavy pink T-shirt that fell to her hips. No shoes or socks. Hidden under the plain clothes and simple hairstyle was a woman with the passion of a lioness.

Suddenly, a heavy sigh issued from her lips, and her shoulders slumped as if she carried the weight of the world. Probably worried about the upcoming recital.

Sam wanted to come up behind her, kiss her nape and make the worries disappear. But doing that would violate their agreement. Instead, he cleared his throat, letting her know he was there. She spun around, straightening her shoulders and lifting her head as she faced him. "That was fast."

He nodded. "Thanks for the use of the shower."

"No problem," she said without quite meeting his eye. "Coffee's about ready. Would you like a cup before you go?"

He wasn't up to sitting around, making small talk. "Better not."

"Okay," she replied, looking relieved.

He shifted awkwardly. "Mariah's parents get

back tomorrow night. Now that the sets are done I probably won't see you again until the night of the recital."

"It's best that way," she said, fiddling with the ends of her braid. "Don't you think?"

"Absolutely."

"You're still going to help backstage, right?"

"I said I would," he muttered.

"You don't have to sound so grumpy about it."

Dammit, he *felt* grumpy. But he was not in the mood to argue, so he let the incendiary comment slide. "I'll be going now."

"I'll see you out."

She unlocked the latch and pulled open the heavy oak door. "Goodbye, Sam," she said.

Her eyes searched his before she bit her lip and stared at her feet. A thick lump formed in his throat. He swallowed hard around it. "Take care, Amy." He started to touch her cheek, then thought better of it.

Before he was down the front steps, the door clicked firmly behind him. Looked as if she couldn't wait to get rid of him. Then what she said was true. Last night had worked for her—she'd gotten him out of her system.

He'd done the same with her, he told himself. *Liar.*

"DID YOU HEAR?" Nina asked the moment Dani answered the phone on Sunday. She'd waited as late as possible to call, but couldn't hold off another moment.

"Hear what?" Dani said.

"Sam was seen leaving Amy's around nine-thirty this morning. I think he spent the night there."

"Really? Whoopee!" Dani shrieked. She covered the mouthpiece but Nina heard everything. "Guess what, Russ? Nina says Sam left Amy's at nine-thirty this morning. He probably spent the night."

"How does she know that?" came Russ's muffled and skeptical comment.

Nina pictured her friend shrugging before she removed her hand from the mouthpiece. "And just how do you know this?" Dani asked.

"Susan Andrews drove past Amy's on her way to church this morning. Get this: she actually saw Sam walk down the front steps and head toward his car. He parked the Porsche right out front. Susan says he needed a shave, so of course he stayed the night. She was worried he'd see her, but doesn't think he noticed her. She said he seemed preoccupied." Nina laughed. "I wonder why? Anyway, Susan phoned Connie from the church phone, then Connie called me around ten."

"Ten! That was a good two hours ago. Why didn't you tell me right away?"

"You're carrying twins," Nina explained. "I wanted you to get your sleep."

"I can do that any time. This is important. It's

Amy we're talking about, our best friend." Dani paused. "I *thought* there was something going on between them. Heck, every time his name came up the other night, she blushed like crazy."

"She wouldn't look at us, either. Wonder why she didn't confide in us?" She thumbed through her dog-eared astrology guide until she found what she sought. "Especially now. Her chart indicates this is a good time to share news with friends."

"I don't know, but I'm real glad she and Sam are seeing each other again." Dani gave a dreamy sigh. "They belong together. She'd better break her date with Bob."

"I'm sure she will. Connie and Bob are friendly enough to talk about who they're dating. She'll find out what she can and let us know."

"Sounds good," Nina said. "Should we call Amy on the three-way?"

"Better not. We don't want to get too pushy, and besides, she's got the recital to worry about. She'll tell us everything when she's good and ready."

"Smart thinking. We'll just sit tight and let the romance unfold."

"Oh, this is so exciting." Nina cupped the receiver between her ear and shoulder so she could rub her hands in glee. "I can't wait to see them together the night of the recital."

MONDAY EVENING, Sam welcomed his sister and her husband back with relief. Between problems with the manager at one of his burger locations, lack of sleep and chauffeuring Mariah around this afternoon, it had been a hell of a day. He looked forward to slipping back into the comfortable role of taking care of himself and nobody else. No more playing Mr. Mom. No car pools and no trips to Amy's studio. He could avoid her as he had before he'd taken charge of his niece. Once he stopped seeing Amy, he had no doubt he'd soon forget her completely. The thought eased the knot of tension that had stayed clamped in his belly since Sunday.

Standing back, he watched the joyful reunion between Mariah and her parents. Despite what she'd said about not really missing them, now that they were home, the kid was ecstatic. From the moment Jeannie and Mike had walked through the door minutes ago, she'd lodged herself like a bullet against her mother's side, only ungluing herself to jump into her father's arms for a welcoming hug.

Though a loved member of the family, Sam wasn't a part of this. He hung back, watching with a pang of envy. At this moment he almost wanted a family of his own.

His thoughts flashed to Amy, but he shook them off. He'd tried the marriage route. It wasn't for him. *She* wasn't for him. She was out of his system, and he was out of hers. He'd repeated that to himself so many times, he almost believed it. And he needed to leave. "I'm sure you're tired," he told his sister and her husband. "So am I, and I want to get home."

Jeannie nodded, her short blond hair bleached almost white by the Hawaiian sun. Unlike Sam, she'd inherited their mother's blond hair and their father's brown eyes. "You handled Mariah's strep throat like a pro. Thanks for that, and everything else, Sam."

"No problemo." He winked at his niece. "We had fun, didn't we kid?"

"Uh-huh." Cuddled between both parents, the girl beamed as she gave a thumbs-up. "Uncle Sam read me stories when I was sick, and we played games, too. He's the best uncle in the world."

"You don't have to tell me," Sam's sister said. She turned to Sam, whose face felt warm with embarrassment. "You managed the driving and car-pooling all right?"

Sam nodded. "I don't know how you do it and practice dentistry. I've gained new respect for you, sis."

"That's one of the reasons I married her," Mike said. Tall and solid as befitted a man who owned his own construction company, he towered over his wife by a full six inches. He shot an adoring look at her. "She can do it all."

"With a little help from my life partner," she replied, smiling fondly at him.

Any fool with eyes could see they were crazy about each other. Lucky couple, Sam thought. Once, long ago, he'd figured he and Amy loved each other that much, but he'd been wrong. Good thing they'd decided to go their separate ways. She needed the right man for her, and it wasn't him. Though at the thought of her with another man, fresh tension knotted his belly. Frowning, he pushed away his thoughts of Amy.

"How was it, seeing Amy?" Jeannie asked in a casual tone that didn't fool Sam. For the past year, she'd hinted that he ought to contact Amy.

Sam shrugged. "It was okay," he said without meeting his sister's eye.

At the mention of her teacher's name, Mariah jumped up and down with a girl's exuberance. "Guess what I found out about Sam and Miss Parker?" she asked her parents.

She looked like the cat with the richest bowl of cream, which put Sam on alert. No telling what she was about to say.

"They used to be married to each other!" Mariah announced with great glee.

Sam rolled his eyes at the ceiling, while Mike covered his mouth with his fist and coughed.

Jeannie's mouth twitched. "We know, honey."

"Oh." Undaunted, the girl gave an impish smile. "I heard some of the moms talking at rehearsal today and they said he still likes her and she—"

Enough was enough. Sam glared at her. "They're wrong," he stated in a forceful tone. "I'd like to glue their gossipy mouths shut."

Mariah gaped at him. "You don't have to yell, Uncle Sam. Geesh. You and Miss Parker were both such grouches today, you didn't even say hello to each other when you dropped me off. How could anybody think you like each other?"

"You got that right." Sam said. "Feel free to set the record straight."

His niece's forehead creased. "If you and Miss Parker don't like each other, how come you're helping her backstage during the recital?"

Mike shot him a curious look. "No kidding?"

"That's awfully nice of you, Sam," Jeannie said with barely concealed excitement.

Given what had happened between him and Amy, Sam wished he could back out. But she needed him, and he'd promised. He shrugged. "She needed someone who wasn't a parent to run interference that night, so I said I'd do it."

"Ah." His sister nodded and exchanged a knowing look with his brother-in-law. Sam didn't like that look.

"Don't go getting any ideas," he warned. "I'm doing it for you two and Mariah. Got that?"

"IT'S A BEAUTIFUL DAY FOR A HIKE," Gabe said as he and Josh tromped into Sam's rec room the following Saturday morning. "Ready to go?"

Their cheery demeanors irritated Sam, who wasn't in the best frame of mind. He gave a listless shrug as he laced up one boot. "I guess."

"You guess?" Gabe stared in disbelief. "It's seventy degrees outside and there isn't a cloud in the sky. You couldn't have planned it any better. And in case you've forgotten, *you* arranged this two months ago."

True, Sam acknowledged, lacing the other boot. But that had been several weeks before he and Amy had run into each other. He hadn't been in a good mood since. "I know. Guess I'm tired."

Gabe scrutinized him with a concerned frown. "It's been several days since your sister and brother-in-law got back. You ought to be recovered from taking care of Mariah by now."

"I am," Sam said. His problems had nothing to do with his niece. "Trouble is, lately I've had problems sleeping." For the past few days, he'd been so restless that he jogged close to eight miles every evening after work, until he felt tired enough to drop. Unfortunately, after a shower and dinner, the edginess returned. He ended up prowling aimlessly around the house until late at night.

Both his friends shot him perplexed glances.

"I'm up to my elbows with this new Cutter's, and that's pumped up my adrenaline level," he explained. Which was true. But not the entire reason for his bad mental state. He couldn't seem to shake free of his need for Amy. He missed her. He wanted her. But he was damned if he'd let those things get him down. They were through with each other and glad of it. Period. Finished with his boots, he stood.

"But we've opened five Cutter's restaurants," Josh said, "and this is no different from any of the others." As Sam's accountant, he knew the drill as well as Sam.

"True, but I still can't sleep."

Gabe studied him appraisingly. "You want to stop by my office Monday for a checkup, to make sure you're okay?"

Sam shook his head. "I haven't been sick in years, and I'm not sick now."

Josh scratched his neck in confusion, while Gabe gave a puzzled shrug.

"He's been in a foul temper all week," Josh told Gabe. "I ought to know, I've met with him and his attorney several times to review the plans for the new Cutter's and put together the real estate deal." He shook his head. "It's been worse than an IRS audit."

"Gee, thanks a lot," Sam muttered. He knew he'd been out of sorts. His short fuse was driving everyone nuts, including himself.

Gabe rubbed his chin with his thumb and forefinger as he scrutinized Sam. "Does your bad mood have anything to do with Amy?"

"Amy?" Sam repeated, stalling for time.

"It's all over town that you spent the night at her place last Saturday night."

Not again. Sam swore. "The busybodies who live here need to find hobbies."

"So it's true," Gabe said. He glanced at Josh, and both men eyed Sam speculatively.

Sam didn't want to go there, but he knew his buddies well. They wouldn't give up until he gave them what they wanted—the truth. He released a hard breath. "Listen, there's nothing between Amy and me, not anymore. We needed to clear up some things, so we, uh, met at her place."

Gabe's brow lifted suggestively. "And your 'meeting' lasted all night long." He grinned and nodded. "Interesting."

"Very." Josh lifted his brows suggestively.

Sam glared from one to the other. "Also none of your business," he snapped.

The accountant held up both hands, palms up. "Okay, okay."

"Whatever," Gabe said. He glanced at Sam. "Given your rotten mood, whatever you were 'clearing up' doesn't seem to have helped."

"Sure it did." For her, anyway. Gabe's mouth was already open again. Before his nosy friend could comment, Sam narrowed his eyes. "This conversation is over."

The doctor nodded. "We were only trying to figure out what's bothering you."

Josh retrieved Sam's day pack from the Barca-lounger. "Maybe he needs to get away from it all. A hike in the woods is just the thing." He tossed Sam the pack. "Let's go."

His friend was probably right, Sam thought as he hooked the strap over his shoulder and followed them out the door. The woods and fresh air couldn't hurt.

Three hours later, they sat beside a gurgling stream in a small clearing, munching on sandwiches and chips, and sipping bottled beer. From the trees surrounding them, birds called out joyously. Color-ful spring flowers dotted the tall spring grass, and a soft, warm breeze stirred the air. Gabe had called it a perfect day, and it was.

Sam enjoyed the outdoors. He should have felt great. Instead, he felt dull and empty. Perched on a warm, flat rock he munched on a chicken salad sandwich Josh's wife had made. His friends had raved about the celery-and-garlic mayonnaise. To Sam, the stuff tasted like cardboard. What in hell was wrong with him?

"…and I told the kid to keep his tongue out of soda bottles," Josh was saying. Chuckling, he shook his head. Gabe laughed heartily. Josh gave Sam a sideways look, and furrows lined his forehead. "You don't think that's funny?"

Sam hadn't heard a word, but didn't feel like ex-plaining. "Nope," he said, clamping his jaw.

Gabe and Josh looked at each other, then turned their attention to Sam.

"Enough already," Josh said. "I can't take any more of your rotten mood, so you'd better start explaining."

Sam tossed aside his lunch. He didn't feel like talking. "I don't have anything to say."

He could tell they didn't buy it. Josh eyed him. "We're your best friends. We're here to help, not judge."

He'd been through hell and back with the two men, and they'd stood by him all the way. But how could he explain what he didn't understand himself? "I don't know," he admitted, kicking at an exposed tree root.

Gabe angled him a look of disbelief. At Sam's blank stare, he shook his head and turned to Josh. "I believe he means that."

Josh hooted, and that really bothered Sam. He didn't hide his feelings. Arms crossed, he narrowed his eyes. "What's so damn funny?"

"You," Josh said. "You're in love with Amy, and you won't admit it."

That was the last thing Sam wanted to hear. "That's a load of bull," he barked as he balled up the remains of his lunch. The birds went silent, a fitting tribute to his wrath. He snatched his day pack from the rock beside him, then shoved his trash inside. "Amy and I are all wrong for each other, and we both know it. We've known it since before the divorce. After the recital I'll never see her again. End of subject," he said, standing. He slung the straps over his shoulders. "I'm ready to head back."

Chapter Twelve

SUNDAY AFTERNOON, Amy stood before the three-way mirror in Nina's tiny dress-making shop, a crowded space crammed with fabric, supplies, sewing machines, an iron and an ironing board. The wedding was fast approaching and with the recital looming, this was the only time to fit Amy's dress.

"The bride really shouldn't get stuck with making the bridesmaid dresses," she said as Nina deftly pulled the cap sleeve, lilac silk taut over her hips.

"I don't mind," Nina replied around a mouthful of pins. "Besides, this way I get exactly what I want." She stopped talking to frown, tug and pin, and for a moment only the oldies song on the radio filled the air. She didn't speak again until she'd emptied her mouth of pins. "I appreciate your taking time this close to the recital for the fitting."

"I needed the break," Amy said. With the recital in less than a week, she'd been going nonstop from dawn to dark. Not that she minded. Work kept her mind off her personal life. Off Sam. She noted the forlorn expression on her face and erased it under a fleeting smile. "I'll be so glad when this recital is over."

Nina frowned at Amy's reflection. "Me, too. Because, no offense, you don't look so good. You've lost weight, and those dark circles under your eyes sure don't flatter you."

"You really know how to make a person feel rotten," Amy muttered. "Even though you're right." She bit her lip. "I haven't been sleeping well lately, and I've lost my appetite, too."

"Stress will do that to you." Another silence while Nina pinned the low-cut bodice. Amy had small breasts, and her friend needed to alter the fit. Intent on the task she didn't speak again until she nodded her approval and moved behind Amy. "Aside from the recital, is anything else bothering you?"

"Not really," Amy hedged. Sam was a man, not "anything." "I cancelled the date with Bob."

"Oh?" Nina poked her head around and eyed Amy's reflection. "What made you change your mind?"

"There's no spark." Unlike the electricity between her and Sam. But then, no one had ever set her heart beating the way he did. Did a man exist who could make her feel as alive as Sam? Since Amy had no future with him, she fervently hoped so. They wanted different things, and were completely wrong for each other.

A frustrated sigh slipped from her lips. How many times must she repeat that before her heart accepted it? The answer was clear—until she got over Sam. In time, she would forget about him. She would.

"Given Bob's reputation, canceling is a wise decision." Nina stood, brushed the threads from the knees of her jeans and, with slightly narrowed eyes, slowly circled Amy, pausing to adjust a pin here and there. "Okay, you can take off the dress now. Just be careful not to poke yourself with those pins."

Grateful to be out of her friend's scrutiny, Amy wriggled carefully out of the dress.

"What's that?" Nina asked, zeroing in on the love bite peeking from the lace edging of Amy's bra.

She'd worn a strapless bra to accommodate the low-cut bridesmaid dress. Unfortunately the thing had inched down, exposing the faded mark just above her nipple. Her cheeks flamed as she reached for her peacock-blue T-shirt and yanked it over her head. "What's what?"

"Don't play dumb with me," Nina said. "Everyone knows Sam spent the night last weekend. And with Venus going into retrograde next month and that dreamy look you get whenever his name comes up, I'd have guessed, anyway."

"Oh." Too downcast to feign surprise or deny her

friend's statement, Amy stepped into her jeans. "As for the dreamy look, you're imagining things. I'm far too levelheaded to fantasize about Sam. What happened between us was…" The words trailed off while she searched for a way to put their intense physical need for each other into words. "Necessary," she finished.

Not that the word even came close to explaining the incredible attraction and unquenchable lust between them. Even now, at the mere thought of the man, her nerves stood primed and eager for more, and her body thrummed. And the depth of intimacy between them…well, it made the loving even more thrilling. For a moment, lost in feeling, she closed her eyes. Then caught herself. She opened her eyes to Nina's frown of concern.

"We did what we needed to do," she added in a calm tone at odds with the emotions whirling inside her. "It's over now, and it will never happen again." The very words caused a hollow ache in her heart.

"Why in the world not?" Nina asked, looking genuinely puzzled. "Neither of you is in a relationship with anyone else," she said as she hung the dress on a padded hanger. "There's no reason for you not to be involved."

"There are several very good reasons," Amy countered. "First," she held up one finger, "Sam doesn't love me." No sense stating the obvious— that she was in love with him. She stepped into her jeans. She trusted Nina, but in a town the size of Forest Hills, even the most confidential information seemed to reach people at the speed of light. If Sam learned that she'd foolishly fallen for him, she'd never be able to look him in the eye again. "Second," she continued, holding up another finger, "you know how badly I want to get married again. He doesn't. He never will."

"How do you know?"

"Because he told me. Sam has always been honest with me, and I'm grateful for that. After the recital, I'll never see him again, except to wave hello on the street."

"But you're miserable," her friend pointed out.

Less than grateful for the reminder, Amy compressed her lips. "I'll be fine," she insisted as she slipped into her clogs. "And I'd appreciate it if we dropped the subject."

AMY WHEELED HER CART rapidly through the near vacant, brightly lit grocery, keenly aware that she had less than thirty minutes to select and pay for groceries. Her fault for showing up at ten-thirty on a Tuesday night. She didn't even want to be here, longed to crawl into bed and close her eyes. But only if that meant no dreams. Unfortunately, for the last week and a half—since that unforgettable night with Sam—her dreams were mostly of him. Often she woke up reaching for him with longing. Of course, he wasn't there, which put her in a wretched mood. So tonight she'd decided to stay up later, hoping that when she finally slept, she'd be too tired to dream. And anyway, with the recital in just four days, there was too much to do to sleep.

And since there was nothing much to eat at home except a few packages of ramen noodles and a block of moldy cheese, she could no longer put off this errand. She hurried from aisle to aisle, piling enough pasta, meats, produce and breads into her cart to last the week. At least by shopping now, she avoided running into nosy friends and townspeople, who mostly shopped for groceries at an earlier hour.

Now to the pharmacy aisle. She needed Band-Aids, bobby pins and hair spray for the recital. Amy ticked off the items as she added them to the cart. Moving forward she glanced at her watch. Seven minutes until closing. She turned the corner, moving toward the magazines. There was still time to pick up— At the sight of the man at the end of the aisle, her thoughts abruptly ended and her step faltered. Sam.

He was angled away from her, rifling through a magazine, but Amy recognized him at once. The broad shoulders and his jet-black hair pulled back at the nape were dead giveaways, not to mention his long legs and very nice rear end. Her heart gave a joyous leap and her breath seemed to catch. Mustering her resolve, she ignored the unwanted elation suddenly lifting her spirits. What was he doing here? It was late, and he should have been at home.

She fleetingly thought about ducking away before he saw her, but that was silly. They were adults, and they were over each other. Forest Hills was a small place. She was bound to run into him now and then, she told herself, forgetting that until a month ago they'd managed to live here for nearly a year without once seeing each other. This was good practice, unencumbered by the eyes of prying townspeople. She just wished she'd changed her clothes, put on makeup and rebraided her hair first.

Determined to act like the mature nearly thirty-year-old woman she was, she pasted a smile on her face and wheeled forward with confidence and poise. She waited to speak until she was almost beside him. "Hello, Sam."

His gaze jerked up from his magazine, a business journal for entrepreneurs. "Amy," he said, clearly surprised.

Warmth flickered in his eyes, and a flush of pleasure washed over her. Abruptly he schooled his expression into the casual indifference of a not-too-close friend.

"What are you doing out so late?" he asked, making polite conversation.

His coolness stung. Amy realized she'd imagined the warmth, maybe because she'd wanted it so much. There was nothing between them, and that was how they both wanted it. She gripped the handle of her cart and forced an easy smile. "With the recital only days away, this is the only time I could squeeze in the shopping."

"I hear that," he said. "I'm about to wrap up negotiations for another Cutter's, and suddenly there's no time for anything else."

That explained the fatigue etched on his face. "Another Cutter's? That's wonderful," she said, meaning it.

"Thanks." Sam nodded.

For a few tense moments they regarded each other, Amy toying with her braid and Sam rolling the magazine between his palms.

Now that she'd run into him, she couldn't wait to get away. Odd, after days and nights spent longing for him. She inched backward. "Well, I should finish shopping before the store closes."

"Me, too," Sam said. "What time should I show up for the recital Saturday night?"

Amy didn't think she could bear seeing him that night. She considered telling him she didn't need his help after all, then quickly nixed that idea. She might be foolish in matters of the heart, but she was no idiot. Sam had agreed to lend a hand and she'd gladly take it. "The performance starts at seven-thirty," she said. "If you could show up an hour before that, I'd appreciate it."

"I'll be there."

"Great," she said brightly. She waved, pivoted her cart around and headed for the dairy section. She had the oddest sensation that Sam was watching her. Feigning interest in the toothpaste she'd just passed, she glanced over her shoulder. He was gone. It had been wishful thinking on her part, nothing more.

Maybe she wasn't over Sam, but he certainly was over her.

Suddenly exhausted, she plodded forward. Tears gathered thickly behind her eyes. She blinked them back. She'd do her crying alone. Repressing her feelings caused an ache in her throat.

Hardly aware of her actions she quickly added eggs, milk, cheese and yogurt to the cart and then headed for the checkout. Right now, she needed to focus all her energy on the upcoming recital. But the minute it was over, she would refocus, doing whatever it took to forget Sam. It was time to move on with her life, meet someone, and settle down.

Otherwise, she'd never survive living in the same town with him.

AS SAM HEADED FROM the parking lot to Amy's studio early Saturday evening, the slanting sunlight nearly blinded him. The irony of that struck him as funny and, shading his eyes, he gave a derisive laugh. He'd been blind, all right, thinking one night with Amy would cure him of wanting her. The joke was on him.

He'd been doing okay until the other night at the grocery. He hadn't been prepared to see her there, and the shock had momentarily waylaid his carefully constructed defenses. He'd been appallingly glad to see her.

Sam recalled the warm look on Amy's face when they'd first locked eyes. For a minute there, he'd almost thought she was glad to see him. But he'd been wrong. She couldn't get away from him fast enough, he recalled. Though he felt exactly the same way, her reaction rankled. He kicked a pebble across the asphalt, watching it skitter angrily into a puddle, the remnant of a heavy rainstorm this afternoon. Too bad his run-in with her had ruined his chances for a good night's sleep. Not that he'd been sleeping all that well anyway.

In the tree overhead, birds chattered noisily. The screeching sounds stabbed annoyingly at his frayed nerves. Muttering an oath, he frowned up at them. Naturally, they paid him no mind. He was tired, irritable and antsy, and sure as hell wished he hadn't agreed to help out tonight. Yet at the same time here he was, heart pounding and palms sweaty, as if he were a kid about to go on his first date.

But this was no date. It was nothing but keeping his word to help with the recital. He didn't want Amy. And she sure as hell didn't want him. His jaw set against the hollow feeling caused by the knowledge.

Even worse, after the recital tonight, she had a date with Bob Swanson.

At the thought, Sam's already low spirits plummeted. Swanson wasn't good enough for her. His reputation as a smooth-talking fast-mover interested in getting a woman into bed made him the wrong man for Amy. Sam imagined the slick bachelor sliding his hands over her. He released a helpless howl and clenched his fists at his sides.

Her love life was none of his business, he sternly reminded himself. After tonight he wouldn't see her again unless they bumped into each other. He would do his job backstage, congratulate his niece and her teacher, and leave. In no time, he'd forget Amy and move on. Squaring his shoulders he strode inside, pausing in the doorway.

Amy stood in the middle of the studio, directing two high school boys who were setting up the folding chairs. She was all dressed up in a softly clinging rose-colored dress and matching heels, her hair twisted into a fancy knot at her nape. The style showcased her long, graceful neck. She looked fragile and beautiful. And nervous, if her fidgeting hands were any indication. Sam forgot about her impending date. A tender feeling he didn't understand swelled his chest. He swallowed and headed forward.

Connie, Kari and Susan—was that her name?— were hunched over a long table placed over the benches, setting out a coffee urn and trays of cookies. Connie noticed him first. She nudged Kari, who elbowed Susan. They glanced from him to Amy. He should have been irritated, but he figured their talk would stop soon enough. When he and Amy no longer saw each other, they'd have nothing to speculate about.

"Hey, Sam," Connie said.

He had time for a quick nod before Amy's attention snapped toward him. "Oh good, you're here."

In another context the pleased expression on her face and the heartfelt words would have filled him with warmth. But he understood her meaning. She needed an extra hand.

"We'll be leaving now," Connie said, pulling Susan and Kari toward the door. "I'm sure the girls need help getting ready."

"Don't be too long," Amy said. "I want them here right away."

As Sam neared her, he was alarmed at what he saw. She was pale, with purple shadows under her eyes. Forgetting to keep his distance, he eyed her with concern. "You okay?"

"Fine." She reached for her braid. But with her hair up, there was no braid. Her hands fidgeted aimlessly, then laced at her waist. "To tell you the truth, I'm a nervous wreck."

Understandable, given that this was her ballet school's very first recital, and that the school and her reputation were on the line.

"How can I help?" Sam asked.

She brightened as if she appreciated his can-do attitude. "If you could change the sets between dances? They're in the storage room, labeled and ready. And before the Pearls go on, you'll need to put out the dry ice, which is in a cooler near the sets. Same for the finale. Also, open and close the curtains when I cue you. Aside from that, hang around backstage. If anyone needs anything, take care of it." She chewed her lower lip. "Okay?"

That sounded easy enough. He nodded. "No problem."

Her mouth relaxed and she let out a loud breath. "Thanks, Sam."

He shrugged. "Glad to help," he said, meaning it.

Piece of cake.

Chapter Thirteen

SAM BARELY HAD time to close the heavy red stage drapes and arrange the set for the first dance before kids started to arrive. Already in costume and makeup, and in high spirits, they passed the time jumping and prancing around backstage, jostling each other and laughing nervously. Through a chink between the curtains, he caught a glimpse of Amy. She'd positioned herself by the door. With a broad smile she greeted parents, family members and guests, and directed her students to the stage. Sam marveled at her composure. If he hadn't talked to her earlier, he'd never have guessed how nervous she was.

Looking shy but cute in her fairy costume, a glittery affair complete with frothy skirt, wings and a sequined crown atop her head, Mariah greeted him with a wave. "Hi, Uncle Sam."

"Uncle?" Pretending confusion, he frowned. "Do I know you?"

His niece tittered. "It's me, Mariah."

"No." Sam rubbed his chin, eyeing her a moment. Then he grinned. "It *is* you. For a minute there, I didn't recognize you. You look beautiful, like a real fairy. Are you nervous?"

She shook her head. "I'm excited." She spotted two female friends and squealed. "I'll see you later." Off she ran. The three beaming girls grabbed hands and jumped up and down.

Sam chuckled at the sight. Soon a chubby boy dressed in the Robin Hood costume all Ruby males wore approached him, carrying a Robin Hood cap. "Can you help me with this, Mr. Cutter?" he asked in the hoarse voice of a boy on the edge of puberty. "I need you to fix it so it doesn't fall off." He unclipped several hairpins from the sleeve of his shirt and offered them to Sam.

Other than when he'd helped Amy take down her hair, Sam had never used a hairpin. But how hard could it be? "Sure," he said, leaning down.

While he did his best to anchor the hat without grazing the boy's scalp, two seven-year-old males raced past him, chased by a giggling girl. A moment later, a loud, clattering crash silenced everyone.

"Oh, no," a voice lamented.

The kid under the hat looked up at Sam. "Uh-oh."

No telling what had happened. "Exactly," Sam muttered. "I used all your pins. Your hat should stay put." He pivoted toward the stage.

The two-dimensional, straw-roof cottage he and Amy had made had toppled to the floor, and the red-faced kids who had raced past him were trying to stand it up.

Sam strode forward. "You kids okay?"

Eyes huge, they nodded in unison. Satisfied that they were fine, Sam quickly righted the house and secured it.

"Did we break it?" the girl asked, popping her thumb in her mouth. She was one of the youngest dancers, a Pearl.

He picked bits of straw from the floor, then gave a reassuring smile. "It looks fine. But no more running," he ordered.

The three kids slunk to the side of the stage, where they joined the forty-one other, now somber, dancers.

Amy suddenly appeared, looking worried and tense. "What happened?"

"It was no big deal," Sam said.

She glanced at her glum students. Bristling protectively, she pivoted toward Sam, her face accusing. "Oh no? Then why do they look so scared?" she demanded in a low but furious tone.

Her anger meant only one thing. She still saw him as he'd been years ago, as a controlling male with rigid expectations and a short fuse. Guilty without a trial. He'd changed and thought she understood that. Apparently not. He stiffened defensively. "Like I said, it's nothing. We're fine."

She glanced again at the now wide-eyed group. "They don't *look* fine."

"Whatever." Jaw clamped, he mentally threw up his hands.

"Uncle Sam didn't do anything," Mariah said in a small voice.

"Some of the kids knocked over the cottage," her friend Janelle added. "Mr. Cutter fixed it."

"Oh." Cheeks red, Amy regarded him. "Guess I overreacted. Sorry."

The apology helped, but not enough to reassure him. Despite everything they'd shared the past few weeks, Amy saw him as the same old Sam. Stung and frustrated, he gave a terse nod. "Go on back to your guests."

When she was gone, he turned to the kids, who seemed upset by what they'd witnessed. This had nothing to do with them. "She's a little stressed," he explained, seeking to reassure.

Several heads nodded and a collective sigh of relief filled the air. "Should we get into our groups now?" Delia Jeffries asked.

Sam didn't have a clue. But the kids looked as if they wanted direction, so he nodded. "Sure."

"Where do you want the Emeralds?" "What about the Rubies and Pearls?" dancers called out, all at the same time.

Hell if he knew, but he had to tell them something. He glanced around the area and quickly decided. "Since the Rubies are on first, you wait here. Emeralds, you wait over there. And Pearls, there."

Chaos ensued but, amazingly, within minutes they stood exactly where he had directed. Sam took advantage of the order to peer again through the slit in the curtains. The seats were filled. He spotted his sister and brother-in-law, talking to Susan Andrews and the man who must be her husband. Kari was there, too.

He saw other familiar faces. It had been years but he recognized Dani and Nina right away. Apple-cheeked and round with her pregnancy, Dani was the picture of health and happiness. And Nina, tall and serene as ever, seemed to glow. The men with them seemed equally content.

There was Bob Swanson. Sam's gaze homed in on the man. Arm draped across the seat beside him, dressed in a sport jacket and shirt open at the throat, he exuded male confidence. Mr. I-Will-Score, Sam thought. Irritation narrowed his eyes. Anyone's guess where the slime planned to take Amy after the recital. At the moment, though, Bob wasn't focused on Amy. Connie sat beside him, and the ex-couple were chatting civilly, friends despite their divorce.

The way Sam and Amy never could be. After what had just happened, he knew that for sure.

AS THE MINUTES TICKED BY, Sam stood concealed behind the curtains on one side, watching along with the now-fidgety dancers for Amy's cue. At last she walked onstage with the poise and grace of a professional performer. If she was nervous, she hid it well. The audience quieted, and she welcomed them and referred them to the printed program for the evening. After a moment, she glanced to the side, where her students waited. "Our first dancers tonight are the Rubies, our eleven- and twelve-year-olds. Let's give them a warm welcome," she said, leading the applause.

While the crowd of family and friends out front clapped, Amy crossed the stage and descended the steps. Standing off to the side, she started the taped music and gave a nod. The sixteen Rubies ran onto the stage in graceful ballet steps.

Sam enjoyed the dance, but didn't get to watch much. A few minutes into the dance, an Emerald a few years Mariah's senior sidled up. "My costume ripped," she whispered in a loud voice. She pointed to her shoulder.

The seam had split open several inches, not enough to matter. Besides, she wore a T-shirt the same color underneath. "It won't show," he told her.

"Yes it will," she insisted with a worried look.

Mariah joined the girl. "You have to fix it, Uncle Sam," she whispered.

Trust his niece to butt in where she wasn't wanted. Sam didn't know much about sewing, and wasn't about to test his skills now. He spoke in a low voice. "How about if I safety-pin it together."

"That'll probably work," the girl said.

He dug through the box of supplies he'd found earlier. Sure enough, there were pins of all sizes. Good thing Amy had stocked it. The girl unbuttoned the top and slipped the sleeve down. With clumsy fingers he pinned the tear. When he finished, she carefully slipped her arm into the sleeve.

"Okay?" Sam asked while the girl buttoned the top.

She looked to Mariah, who nodded. "Thanks," the girl said.

He didn't have time to draw a relieved breath before the music ended and it was time to change the set. As he dragged the trees he and Amy had cut out and decorated across the wood floor, he heard muffled sobs.

What now? Quickly he placed the pieces. Then, following the soft wailing, he found the source of the tears. The small girl who, with her friends, had knocked over the cottage prop sat on the floor, covering her face with her hands. Her two male buddies and several girls patted her on the back, but she did not seem comforted. Sam hunkered down beside her. "What's the matter, honey?"

She peeked through her fingers at him. "I c-can't remember my part."

Totally out of his realm, he squeezed her narrow little shoulder awkwardly. "Sure you can."

She sniffled. "Nuh-uh."

To Sam's dismay, her friends looked as if they, too, would cry.

What to do? He thought fast. "Miss Parker's right out front. If you forget what to do, she'll remind you."

"How can she do that?" a red-haired girl asked. "She's not talking."

"Right, but she mouths the steps. Look." He parted the curtain a fraction and the kids peeked out. Just as he had said, Amy stood with her back to the audience, silently mouthing the dance steps. She looked the picture of a nurturing teacher. Sam felt a rush of pride. "See what I mean?" he murmured in a low voice.

After a minute, the girl and her friends nodded. Sam pulled a tissue from a box nearby and handed it to her. "Going to be okay now?"

Another nod.

"Except she needs new makeup," the red-haired girl pointed out in a soft voice.

Sam rolled his eyes. Great. "Anybody here know how to put on makeup?"

"Janelle and I can," his niece volunteered.

He nodded. "Go to it."

No sooner had the strains of a new song started than a sturdy-looking boy lunged for the wastebasket. "I think I'm going to be sick," he groaned. Right then and there, he threw up.

Despite the performance on stage, girls shrieked, and boys called out, "Ew, gross."

Though the music was loud, everyone heard. People murmured and craned their necks.

"Shh." Sam pressed his finger over his mouth and the dancers sheepishly nodded.

He handed the kid a tissue and watched as he wiped his mouth. "You okay, son?"

"Now I am."

Sam nodded. The Emeralds' part of the recital was halfway over. He figured he had time to get rid of the mess before the next set change. "I'll be back," he told the kids. "You stay put."

Careful to remain hidden, he crouched behind the set and slipped offstage from the side. He carried the receptacle to the bathroom, emptied and rinsed it out. Now the dance was nearly finished, and there was no time to waste. Sam returned the way he'd left.

By the time he rejoined the students, the boy who had thrown up and the tearful girl were bouncing with energy at the edge of stage, awaiting their turn.

In the brief lull between dances, Sam quickly adjusted the set, leaving the trees in place and positioning the moon, clouds and glittering gauze scrim Connie and others had made. With moments to spare, he placed dry ice along the bases of the trees. "Smoke" began to fill the stage floor, creating a magical effect.

The music Mariah had practiced to began and the Pearls danced onto the stage. From his place at the side, he watched, paying special attention to his niece. Smiling as Amy had schooled them, the youngest group danced out of sync, but looked very proud.

One more set change, complete with a replenishment of dry ice, and the entire group returned to the stage for the finale. Suddenly, in what seemed no time at all and at the same time forever, the performance ended.

As each group took their bows, Sam and the parents applauded wildly. Spent, he sagged against a wall backstage. He ran a thriving business, juggling numerous tasks at one time. But this was by far the hardest job ever. Amy worked with these kids nearly every day. How did she do it? Despite the fact that she thought little of him, his admiration for her grew.

The dancers beckoned to Amy. She walked onto the stage. Beaming, she gestured to the group. Fresh applause followed. Dancers from each group handed her colorful bouquets. With her arms full, she dipped her head in thanks. She looked pleased and glad it was over at last.

"I'd like to thank Sam Cutter for his help backstage," she said when the applause died. She gestured to him to join her.

The last thing he wanted was to stand there in front of everyone, but he couldn't refuse her. Not in her moment of success. Feeling self-conscious, he strode forward. Turning toward him, she executed a graceful ballet curtsy. Sam bowed in acknowledgment. Everyone cheered.

Amy held out her arm, offering her hand. Her grip was firm and warm. Though it was only for show, a heady rush of pleasure filled him. He couldn't resist a glance at Bob, who threw him a thumbs-up. Sam puzzled over that, but could make no sense of it.

Releasing his hand, she again addressed the audience. "Thank you all for your support tonight and throughout this first year of the Amy Parker School of Dance."

She listed the volunteers by name, then invited everyone to enjoy the treats provided by generous parents. Conversation buzzed. Kids made a beeline for the food, leaving Sam and Amy alone onstage.

"Congratulations on a job well done," he said over the noise.

"Thanks." Her face was still flushed with pleasure. "I couldn't have managed tonight without your help."

The words sounded right, but Sam knew the truth. She'd wrongly assumed he wanted to control her students. She didn't believe he'd changed, didn't really trust him and had only asked for his help because she wanted the parents out front, watching. There'd been no one else to ask. Dammit, that hurt, and he gave a derisive snort. "Well, you got what you wanted."

Her eyes widened. Coloring, she bit her lip. "Sam, I—"

"Miss Parker, come and meet my cousin," a student called.

Her gaze sought his. "I'd better go. Find me later, will you?"

He shrugged. What more was there to say? In any case, she was leaving with Bob. Sam didn't want to stick around for that. He'd find his sister, her husband and Mariah, then leave.

He ambled down the stage steps and pushed through the crowd, until he located his family sitting on a bench. "Great dancing, kid," he said.

His niece looked up from a plate heaped with treats. Despite a mouthful of cookies, she managed a grin.

"We're so proud of her," Jeannie said.

"We sure are." Mike beamed. "She told us what a great job you did behind the scenes."

Sam wasn't good at taking compliments. "Thanks," he said, shoving his hands into his pockets.

"Come over for dinner tomorrow night?" Jeannie asked.

"Sure." Ready to go, he turned toward the door.

From out of nowhere, Bob appeared. "Hey there, Sam." He clapped a hand on Sam's shoulder. "Good job backstage."

Sam shrugged out of his grip. "It went okay."

"Amy seemed to appreciate it." Bob winked. "I think she likes you." He licked his lips. "Wish I'd volunteered to work back there."

Sam reacted without thinking, leaning to within inches of the other man's face. "Keep your dirty hands off her," he snarled.

Bob held up his hands and backed away. "Easy, man," he said with wide eyes. "It's only talk."

"Offensive talk," Sam retorted. "Amy's too good for that." He narrowed his eyes. "She's way too good for you."

"I don't know about that," Bob said. "But you can relax. We're not going out tonight, or ever. She broke the date."

Sam's jaw dropped as relief sluiced through him. "I didn't hear about that."

"Well, it's true." Bob straightened his shirt and offered a humorless smile. "Can't win them all."

"Amy just did," Sam said. Elated, he pivoted away from Bob and the exit as he searched the crowd for her. Only to praise her on using good judgment, he assured himself.

But parents and friends were gathered around her, and he only caught glimpses of her. Sam hesitated. Since she considered him too controlling, she'd no doubt think he was gloating because she'd followed his advice. Better to leave things as they were.

Goodbye, Amy. Swallowing past a sudden lump in his throat, he strode through the door without looking back.

AS PARENTS AND STUDENTS trickled out, Amy at last had a chance to breathe. She wanted to find Sam and apologize for jumping all over him earlier. Frayed nerves had sapped her patience. She'd accused him of being rigid and controlling toward her students when he hadn't.

She surveyed the room and the approximately twenty remaining people, but there was no sign of him. Kari and Connie were cleaning up the refreshment table, and she approached them. "Thank you both for your help tonight."

"Any time," Kari said as she wrapped leftover cookies in plastic wrap. "It was a wonderful recital."

Amy gave a gratified smile. "I'm so glad you enjoyed it."

Leaning down, Connie unplugged the coffee urn. "I think it was real smart of you to cancel that date with my ex," she said when she straightened. "He's not what I'd call good dating material."

"So I've heard." Amy glanced around the nearly empty room once more. "Have either of you seen Sam?" The two women shared a look she didn't like. "I wanted to thank him again for his help," she explained.

Kari shrugged. "I think he left, didn't he, Connie?"

The blonde nodded. "Shortly after the recital ended."

Without a goodbye? "Oh," Amy said. She tamped down her disappointment. She'd wanted a last chance to talk, to wish each other luck and smooth over what had happened earlier. She'd wanted closure so they each could go on with their lives.

That wasn't going to happen.

Maybe ending things this way was for the best. Amy didn't believe that, but she really had no other option. Sam was gone. His choice, and she couldn't change it. Suddenly, for no reason she could discern, her life stretched before her bleak and empty. She chalked that up to fatigue and the letdown after the performance.

Connie and Kari were studying her openly. She offered a tiny smile. "I don't know about you, but I'm exhausted. I'll finish cleaning up tomorrow." She planted a hand on each woman's shoulder and guided them to her office, where they'd stowed their purses. "Let's call it a night."

If Sam wanted things to end this way, so be it.

Tomorrow was a new day, the start of her life without him. Her heart ached as if it had broken in her chest. She bit back a sob of despair. She'd survived before and she could do it again.

No matter how much it hurt.

Chapter Fourteen

"A SPA BACHELORETTE party is the best!" Nina beamed as Amy, Nina, Dani and six of Nina's friends padded barefoot and robed from the dressing room.

"This was Amy's idea," Dani said, adjusting the robe over her bulging belly.

Amy nodded. "With only nine days until the wedding, I figured you needed a chance to relax."

She'd come up with the plan just before the recital three-plus weeks ago. Each woman had taken the afternoon off and driven to Seattle for a full three hours of pampering, followed by a gourmet dinner.

At the time, it had seemed a great way to celebrate the waning days of Nina's single status. But at the moment, Amy couldn't muster up much enthusiasm. Lately, nothing excited her.

"I'm going to try the seaweed wrap and then a full body massage," Nina announced.

"And I'm heading for a pedicure and foot massage," Dani said. "Since I can barely see my toes, I'm really looking forward to this."

Everyone laughed.

Each woman wanted to indulge in something different, and Amy half listened as they discussed the various procedures. Finally, Nina glanced her way. "You're awfully quiet, Amy. What are you going to try?"

"I haven't decided yet."

"You don't sound so eager."

She forced a lively grin. "Oh, but I am. I'll get the wrap and then the massage, just like you."

Half an hour later, she lay on a narrow table beside Nina, while the uniformed masseuse worked wonders on her hip. Of course, she wasn't as good as Sam… Amy's heart contracted, as it did whenever she thought of him. Which, for a woman bent on finding the man of her dreams, was far too often. With firm resolve, she emptied him from her mind.

When the massage ended, Nina released a relaxed sigh. "I feel marvelous," she proclaimed.

"Me, too," Amy lied.

Apparently with less zeal than Nina expected. She frowned. "Is anything wrong?"

Amy shook her head. "I think I'll head for the showers."

"But we've only been here ninety minutes. We're

booked for another hour and a half," Nina said. "We still need facials and manicures and hot waxes on our legs."

It sounded wonderful, but Amy couldn't muster the energy for more. "You go ahead," she said. "I'll find you later."

"Okay." Looking disappointed and confused, Nina headed off.

Eyes on the white tile floor, Amy shuffled toward the dressing room. Dani suddenly appeared at her side. "What is the matter with you?" she hissed in a low voice. "Your bad mood is ruining Nina's bachelorette party."

Amy stared at her in surprise. Dani rarely got angry. Apparently this was one of those times. "I'm sorry. I didn't realize." Contrite, she bit her lip. "I guess I'm just letting down."

Concern replaced Dani's fiery frown. "You've been 'letting down' since the recital three weeks ago. It was a smash success. The whole town's talking about it, and a ton of kids have signed up for classes in the fall. This is what you wanted."

Amy shrugged, knowing she should feel elated. "I know."

Her friend scrutinized her through narrowed eyes. "How was that blind date with that banker the other night?"

A friend had set Amy up, but at the last minute she'd canceled. "I didn't go."

"But you said you wanted to start dating after the recital. You were going to work on finding a husband full-time, remember?"

"Of course I remember," Amy said. Right now she just didn't have the heart for it. "I'll start dating soon, I swear."

Another odd look from Dani. "Maybe you're sick, or something. How long has it been since your last physical?"

"A few months." Amy met her eye. "There's not a thing wrong with me." Except for the hole where her heart used to be.

"Could have fooled me." Dani pursed her lips. "For Nina's sake, at least pretend to be happy."

Amy nodded. Pasting a bright smile on her face, she lifted her head. "How about that facial?" she said.

JOSH ANGLED HIS CHIN toward Sam and gave a frown of concern. "What's wrong, Sam? You just scored a prime piece of real estate for a bargain price. This is what we've been working for, for weeks. You should be happy."

Sam forced a smile. "I am."

Except for the empty feeling in his chest. It had been there for three weeks, since the night of the recital. In all honesty, it had been there since the morning after making love with Amy.

"You need a woman." Josh advised. "Why don't

you stop off at Bill's Pub on the way home and hook up with someone?"

Sitting in a singles bar, scoping out females was the last thing Sam felt like doing. But, hell, anything was better than an evening alone with his thoughts. His foul mood was making it difficult to stand his own company. He shrugged. "Why not?"

His friend nodded and gave a thumbs-up. "I want to hear about it tomorrow."

Who knew? Sam thought. He just might meet the woman who could take his mind off Amy. Yet he drove toward the tavern with all the enthusiasm of a convicted man headed for the gallows. Truth be told, he wasn't interested in meeting a new woman.

He wanted Amy.

Tough. That was over.

His brain knew that, but his heart hadn't figured it out yet. Passing the tavern without slowing down, he headed straight home for another long and lonely night.

"SHOULD DANI AND I BE HERE?" Nina asked over the country song wailing from the jukebox. It was Thursday night, and Gabe and Josh had invited them to Bill's Pub for a meeting. "I mean, this is really none of our business."

"Not true," Josh said. "When your best friends are miserable and too stubborn to admit they're ruining their lives, their problems become our business."

"You are so right," Dani agreed with a sober nod. "We need a plan."

"Which is why we asked you and Dani to meet," Gabe said.

Josh hoisted his glass. "To interfering for the sake of your friends."

They all tipped their drinks—beer for Nina, Gabe and Josh, and sparkling water for Dani—and sipped. Then they settled down to serious conversation.

After a while, they agreed on a plan. "Friendship or not, Amy's going to kill us when she hears about this," Nina warned. "Want to bet that Sam will, too?"

"We're about to find out." Josh pointed his chin toward the door. "He just walked in."

WHAT WERE HIS FRIENDS UP TO? Sam wondered as he shouldered open the Bill's Pub old wooden door. The smells of smoke, beer and pizza greeted him, accompanied by a whiny country music song. Just what he needed, a song about some guy's broken heart.

Gabe had phoned this afternoon, asking Sam to meet him and Josh here. That had put him on alert. Not that meeting his friends for an occasional beer was unusual. But on a week night, at a singles' bar? Both were family men, they got together when their wives were busy or they brought their wives along. If they were trying to fix him up with someone…

Squinting in the dim light Sam searched out his friends. Since it was a weeknight, there wasn't much of a crowd, making it easy for him to spot them. They'd taken a booth in the back corner. Sam headed straight for them.

What wasn't so easy was trying to figure out who they were with. Two women Sam didn't recognize, at least not from the backs of their heads. They weren't spouses, which puzzled Sam even more. Then they both turned toward him. Dani and Nina.

What were they doing here, and why were they with Gabe and Josh? The guilty expressions on the women's faces and his buddies' sheepish looks forewarned Sam that he'd been set up. He didn't know how or why just yet, but he was sure that, want to or not, he'd find out soon. His gut bunched with dread, and he didn't bother to conceal his annoyance.

"Hey, Sam," Dani said. Nina waved her fingers at him.

He nodded stiffly, then scowled at Gabe and Josh. "What's going on here?"

"Sit down and have a beer," Josh said. "Then we'll explain."

The men slid over, making room. Gabe filled a mug and skated it across the shiny wood table. Though Sam didn't plan to stay, he sat down. He ignored the beer. "I'll give you five minutes, then I'm out of here."

His seatmates glanced at one another. Gabe eyed

Josh, who shrugged and aimed his attention on Dani. "You want to start?"

"Gladly." She attempted to lean forward, but her pregnant belly stopped her. Elbow on the table and chin propped in her palm, she eyed Sam. "First, we're here because we care about you and Amy."

"Or because you're damn nosy," Sam snorted. His four seatmates shifted uneasily.

"Second," Dani continued, shifting her head to the other palm, "you should know that Amy isn't aware of this meeting. She'd have fits if she knew." She paused to regard him with frank openness. "Though in all honesty, having a fit doesn't begin to describe Amy's state of mind. She's a total wreck."

"And not just because she's got a Mars-moon opposition right now," Nina cut in.

Sam scoffed at that. For some reason, he also felt the need to defend Amy. "The first year of her ballet school just ended. That recital was a huge responsibility," he said, shooting them an are-you-all-morons? frown. "It takes time to wind down from that."

"I think we all realize that," Nina replied, clearly offended at his tone. "Now, as Dani was trying to explain…" She glanced at Dani. "May I?" The pregnant woman nodded. Nina leaned her tall frame forward and came straight to the point. "Amy's a miserable mess, Sam, and you're the only person who can help. You see, she's in love with you."

That couldn't be true. Amy had said she'd gotten him out of her system. She'd acted no different the night of the recital, in fact had called him controlling. He certainly hadn't heard from her or seen her. "No she's not," he said. "She doesn't like me at all."

"Not true. You're the only man she wants."

For the first time in weeks, hope stirred in his chest. He eyed Nina warily. "And she told you this?"

"Of course not! She'd never admit to caring for you. She's too darn stubborn, as hardheaded as…as you, Sam."

He frowned. "Me, hardheaded? That's a crock of—"

"Will you please just think about it?" Dani interrupted. She shot him a quelling look, and then Gabe and Josh did, too.

Sam grumbled, then gave up and scratched the back of his neck. "You're jumping to the insane conclusion that Amy has feelings for me—a totally misguided assumption."

"There's nothing insane or misguided about it," Nina huffed. "Dani and I know Amy as well as we know ourselves. She does love you, Sam, totally and completely. She's just confused. Or maybe scared. Or both. And, like I said, too stubborn to admit it."

Amy loved him. Or so they said. Sam had seen no evidence of that, but then, he'd never been able to think clearly around her. Truth be told, hadn't been able to think clearly since that night in her bed. Too stunned to speak, he opened his mouth. Closed it.

Gabe took over the conversation. "You're in the same boat, buddy. You're head-over-heels for Amy. I'd stake my life on that."

The last time his friend had spelled out Sam's feelings, he had angrily denied it. Now he conceded that Gabe just might be right. "Maybe I am," he admitted glumly. "And maybe Amy has feelings for me, too. But what difference does it make? We're all wrong for each other, and we both know it. We've known it since our divorce a dozen years ago."

"That's where the stubborn part comes in," Nina said, enunciating slowly as if he were ten years old. "Neither of you will admit that you've both changed."

"That's true, buddy," Josh added. "You've come a long way, and from what Nina and Dani tell me, so has Amy."

The women nodded.

"If you love her and she loves you, you owe it to each other to give your relationship a chance," Nina said. "Otherwise, my wedding—which happens to be coming up a week from Saturday—will be one melancholy event. As a bridesmaid, Amy plays an important part in the ceremony. If she's unhappy, the whole event will be. I don't want to start my marriage on a sad note."

"And what about the twins?" Dani cupped her belly. "They should know Amy as the lovely, warm woman she's meant to be, not a person going through the motions of living."

"For your own mental health and ours, one of you has to give in." Gabe pushed a half eaten bowl of peanuts back and forth over the shiny, wooden table. "We figured it should be you, Sam."

With all four faces focused intently on him, Sam found it difficult to think. He stared into his untasted beer and considered his friends' conversation. Like it or not, what they said made sense. Maybe, just maybe, he and Amy had a future together. The thought lifted his spirits the way nothing else could. But he'd been burned badly before. He wasn't about to rush into anything. He returned his attention to his friends. "I'll think about it."

"Don't think too long or you and Amy will wind up both miserable *and* friendless," Nina commented wryly.

Chapter Fifteen

FRESH FROM HIS morning shower, Sam stood before the bathroom mirror to shave early Saturday morning. Even with half his face hidden in lather he looked like hell, with his eyes red from lack of sleep and his mouth at a mournful slant. Unfortunately, he felt even worse than he looked. His friends knew why, had risked his anger in an attempt to point out what Sam in his dejected state had refused to acknowledge: that he loved Amy and that, just maybe, she cared for him.

They were right about one thing, he conceded as he shaved. He loved her, wanted her and needed her in his life. Should he tell her how he felt, risking rejection and heartbreak? Could he be the husband she needed? Equally important, did he possess the patience and nurturing qualities he needed to be a decent father to their children?

With each question, the razor slicked over his cheeks, leaving swaths of clean skin in its wake but no answers. He was sick of himself, tired of his indecision and bad mood. On automatic pilot, he rinsed the blade and started on his chin. Damned if he didn't nick himself. He swore, his voice startlingly loud in the silence. At least he wasn't bleeding—on the outside, anyway.

He finished the job in a funk. Nothing could be worse than this miserable state of limbo. He stared at the mirror, and suddenly the words slipped out. "I love her," he said. "I love Amy Parker."

The words resounded in his chest and echoed through the tiled room. And just like that, he made up his mind. It was time to take action, take the chance of a lifetime.

It was time to tell Amy how he felt.

The thought both exhilarated and scared him. What if she rejected him? He swallowed hard, imagining the pain. But if there was the slightest chance their friends were right, that Amy loved him, too, they owed it to each other to see where that led. In any case, he couldn't survive another day without talking to her. This was a risk worth taking, even at the crack of dawn. The decision lifted an invisible weight from his shoulders.

He knew exactly what to do. He'd bring her here. Except for his family and friends, he'd never brought a woman into his house. For some reason, it was important to show it to Amy.

Once again, his spirits lifted. He studied his reflection, noting the determination that now bright-

ened his expression. He gave himself a thumbs-up
and a grin.

Whistling, he dressed quickly, slid into the
Porsche and sped toward Amy's place.

AMY STARED UP AT THE yellow plaster ceiling in her
bedroom. It was not quite dawn Saturday morning,
and exactly one week before Nina's wedding. She
should have been excited, or at least mildly enthusiastic, about her friend's marriage. Instead, here she
was, as gray as the early morning sky, a colorless ball
of misery. Her pity party had nearly ruined Nina's
bachelorette party. She would not let it ruin the wedding. It was time to put an end to the moping, time
to come to grips with the truth and move ahead with
her life.

First, the facts. Eyes closed, she reviewed them
in her mind. Want to or not, and against her better
judgment, she loved Sam. She'd tried to forget him,
but it wasn't happening. He owned her heart, and
nothing could change that.

Those were the facts. Now, what was she going
to do about it?

Tell him.

A scary idea, for he could easily reject her. At
that unbearable thought, Amy hugged her pillow
hard against her chest. Yet the notion of sharing her
feelings with Sam grabbed hold of her and wouldn't
let go.

Suddenly she had to see him, right now. Her mind spinning, she sat up and glanced at the clock. It was way too early to wake him up. She'd wait a few hours, then drive to his house and explain how she felt. She would tell Sam she loved him.

Energized by her decision, she sprang out of bed. After a quick bath, she dressed. She tried to swallow a cup of coffee, but she was too nervous. Forget breakfast. She checked the time again. Exactly half an hour had passed since she'd made her momentous decision. Still too early, but she could wait no longer.

Car keys in hand she hurried toward her door. As she grabbed the knob, someone knocked. At this hour, who could it be? She frowned, then opened it. *Sam.* Oh, it was good to see him. Her heart lifted.

"Sam," she said. "I was just headed to—"

"I know it's early, but can I have an hour of your time?" he interrupted, shifting nervously.

Despite the anxiety that tightened his shoulders and his jaw, a determined glint flashed in his eyes. Amy decided to hear him out and then share her own thoughts. She gestured him inside.

He shook his head. "I'd like you to come with me."

At this hour? "Where?" she asked, puzzled.

"I'd rather just show you. Please." He shuffled his feet over the welcome mat while rubbing the back of his neck, reminding her of a self-conscious boy on his first date. "But if you'd rather not…"

The uncharacteristic self-doubt intrigued her. "I'll come."

He took her hand and pulled her down the steps. Neither of them spoke on the short drive. Sam trained his gaze on the road, now and then darting nervous glances her way. Amy was on edge, too, and preoccupied with her thoughts. Regardless what he said or did, she would stick to her plan, tell him the truth— that she loved him. Her stomach seemed to turn over on itself. God willing, he wouldn't reject her.

He turned into a cul-de-sac of expensive homes on large view lots. She recognized the name of the street—Sam's street. Why bring her here? He pulled into a winding, wooded drive, driving slowly toward the modern glass-and-cedar home ahead.

The moment the car rolled to a stop, he turned to her. "I'd like to show you my home," he said, almost shyly.

She sensed that this was important to him. It felt important to her, too. Her heart thudded in her chest. "I'd like to see it."

He took her on a quick tour of the four-bedroom, custom-designed home, ending in the spacious great room that overlooked a large backyard and the private lake beyond. Standing before a floor-to-ceiling window, she turned to him with wonder. "It's beautiful, Sam."

"Thanks." Holding his gaze on the sweeping view, he gave a gratified nod.

Tension radiated from him, making her even more nervous. Was this all, then? Just a tour and silence?

Unable to stem her curiosity a moment longer she spoke. "Why did you bring me here?"

At last he looked at her, his expression somber. "My home has always been my private haven, off-limits to all but my family and select friends. But now… The thing is, it's too big for just one… I've been… I can't… Hell." Clearing his throat, he rocked back on his heels. "I'm nervous, so bear with me."

He was cute when flustered, but Amy wisely refrained from saying so. Besides, her heart was in her throat and she could barely speak. She nodded as in, *I'm listening.*

He cleared his throat again. "I may as well just come out and say it." Cupping her shoulders, he searched her eyes. "I love you, Amy, and I can't live without you."

Stunned, she gaped at him. "Run that by me again."

"I love you," Sam repeated. "I've changed, I swear it. Will you give me a chance to prove it?"

Tears filled her eyes. "Oh, Sam, if only you knew. I was on my way here to tell you that I'm in love with you. And to apologize for what I said at the recital. You don't have to prove a thing. I know you've changed."

It was his turn to look pleasantly surprised. "Really?"

She bit her lip and nodded. "We both have. I love you, Sam."

His eyes, too, filled. His hands shook as he touched her face. "Then this is one lucky day for both of us."

For a long moment, they studied each other with watery smiles. Then Sam sobered. "Do you think you could live here?"

"You mean, sell my house?"

He shrugged. "If you'd rather I move in with you, that's fine by me. I'll sell this place, instead."

Amy knew Sam's home meant a great deal to him. "You'd do that for me?" she asked.

"I like your house. Besides, I could live in a shack, just as long as we're together." He warmed her with a tender smile. "Will you marry me—again?"

Amy could hardly believe what she'd heard. She shook her head as if shaking cotton from her ears. "But, I thought you didn't want marriage."

"Like I said, I've changed. This time, I want a partner, an equal."

Amy hesitated. She wanted to marry him. But what if they fell into the same pattern that had destroyed their marriage before? Her doubts must have shown, for Sam frowned.

"We're adults. Let's get everything out in the

open, no holds barred." He pulled her toward the sofa, and they sat down. He regarded her intently. "Talk to me, Amy."

The encouragement in his eyes told her he wanted to hear whatever she had to say, that he would listen without growing defensive or angry. It was wonderful, knowing she could voice her deepest concerns. "What about my career?" she asked, holding her breath despite herself.

His warm smile put her at ease. "I know how important dance is to you." Taking her hands, he looked her straight in the eye. "You have my word that I'll support you every way possible."

She believed him. Relief rushed through her. There was one more important topic to discuss. "I want children, hopefully a houseful," she said, watching his face. "How do you feel about that?"

He didn't shy away from her scrutiny. "I've been thinking that over. I'll probably make my share of mistakes, but overall I believe I'll make a pretty good father." He grinned. "To tell you the truth, I can't wait to make babies with you. I see us as a team. We'll work, support each other and share the child-rearing. With all the love in our home, our children will be the luckiest little people in the world."

The words expanded her heart. Amy bit her lip and glanced around the spacious room. "You know, this *is* a perfect house for children."

Sam nodded. "With four bedrooms, it's big enough. The woods and the lake make it a kids' paradise. It's a great place to raise a family. Our family, if you want." He met her gaze with hopeful expectation.

"I do." As she cupped Sam's face between her hands Amy's eyes filled again. "Yes, Sam, I'll marry you."

He whooped. "All right!"

Then he kissed her. Heat and warmth flooded her, along with the glorious feeling that she'd just made the best decision of her life.

When her bones had turned to mush, Sam broke the kiss. He stood, pulling her with him. "I happen to have a drawer full of condoms in my bedroom upstairs…."

"So you planned this?" she teased, remembering the last time they'd made love.

"Always be prepared. That's my motto." He grinned. "At least until after the wedding. Then I'll toss the birth control."

Side by side, they headed upstairs, where Amy showed Sam just how much she loved him.

Epilogue

Eleven months later

AMY PARKER CUTTER cupped her pregnant belly and stood before her class. "Attention, Pearls, Rubies and Emeralds! Rehearsal for the recital's finale starts soon. First, though, I have a surprise." She smiled at Sam, who had just walked through the door with several teenage assistants.

He returned the smile, and even from thirty feet away, she felt the warmth in his eyes. "Because you've all worked so hard on the recital, Mr. Cutter and I thought you deserved a treat. He's brought milkshakes from Cutter's."

The children shrieked with surprise and excitement, Mariah's voice loudest of all. Mouth cocked in a grin, Sam and his helpers strode forward. Amy directed the group to line up. Sam paid the assistants and they left. While the kids enjoyed their treat, he hustled Amy into her small office.

He shut the door, then kissed her soundly. "Hi, you."

"Hi," she returned, unable to tear her eyes from his. How she adored him.

"How's the baby this afternoon?"

"She's kicking like crazy. I think she'll be a dancer."

"Just like her mama." Sam patted her belly lovingly. "I wouldn't have it any other way."

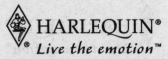

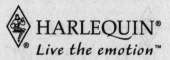

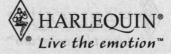

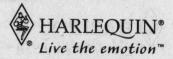

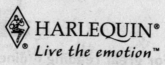

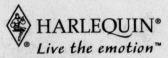